Praise for Michael Scott Moore's
Too Much of Nothing

"A taut, gripping tale of murder animated by rabbi-wisdom and Reagan-era pop culture, *Too Much of Nothing* is a smart, vibrant, and utterly original novel. Rastafarians and Goths, Colombian coke and R.E.M., Cheez-Its and the Zohar intermingle in this '80s So-Cal landscape, but Moore does more than dazzle us with a clever pastiche—he tenderly excavates the heart of an adolescent haunted by angst and longing."
—Rebecca Donner, author of *Sunset Terrace*

"*Too Much of Nothing* is a sometimes funny story about a sensitive ghost who, as a very much alive teenager, tried but failed to enjoy the Dead Kennedys, good blow, and sex. There is more to enjoy in this book about nothing—absence, nonexistence, and an insomniac ghost—than there is to enjoy in five novels with characters weighted in flesh." —Joe Loya

"Michael Scott Moore has a remarkable understanding of the type of teenager who becomes achingly self-aware while still trapped in the confines of adolescence. He knows the cruelties meted out by children to other children, the bizarreness of first sexual encounters, the offhanded betrayal of friends. Moore chillingly (and sometimes comically) chronicles the frantic forms of self-destruction to which such teenagers, like other caged creatures, are prone."
—Ethan Watters, author of *Urban Tribes: A Generation Redefines Friendship, Family, and Commitment*

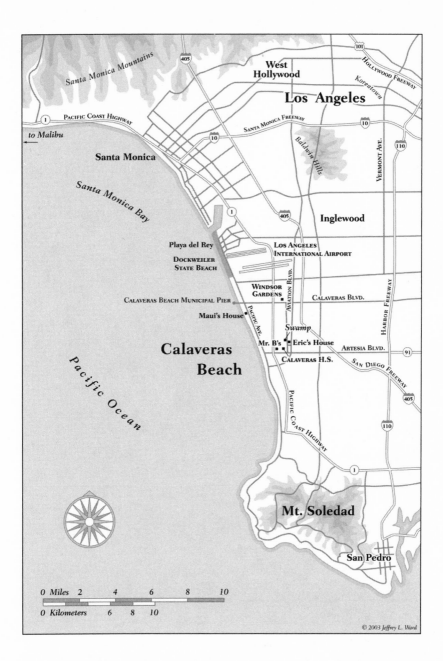

© 2003 Jeffrey L. Ward

too much of nothing

michael scott moore

CARROLL & GRAF PUBLISHERS
NEW YORK

TOO MUCH OF NOTHING

Carroll & Graf Publishers
An Imprint of Avalon Publishing Group Inc.
161 William St., 16th Floor
New York, NY 10038

Library of Congress Cataloging-in-Publication Data is available.

ISBN: 0-7867-1196-5

Printed in the United States of America
Distributed by Publishers Group West

For Dr. Richard Mitchell, 1929-2002

Irreverent and fiery Lincoln of the mind, who knew the real
meaning of "adolescent literature"

too much of Nothing

Ev'rybody's doin' somethin',
I heard it in a dream
But when there's too much of nothing,
It just makes a fella mean

—Bob Dylan, "Too Much of Nothing"

i

The graveyard where my bones are buried lies close enough to the beach to receive a shroud of fog on mornings when the chill breath of the ocean rolls onshore. I like to linger in the fog, hang around like a scrap of it, and listen to the slapping waves. Sometimes I'll wander to the beach and watch the homeless men who live there like phantoms, browsing trash cans for clothing and food. I'll sit on the concrete steps leading down from the strand and explain myself to a dirty, wire-bearded man with shining eyes, a lunatic more interested in some half-eaten sandwich than in my grievances, who, as a general rule, will turn away before I'm done and go grumbling into the fog. It's frustrating. To the most observant or sensitive people I must be nothing more than a shimmer of air, an unexotic wave of heat, but I can feel the dimensions of my body the way amputees can feel their missing arms or legs. I still have the stubborn sense of being Eric Sperling, mopey shlemielish teenager, walking around in baggy shorts and a digital watch. In fifteen years, this feeling hasn't dissipated. My nerve-illusion, or whatever it is—this wispy shape—has grown heavier, to the point where I'm not even convinced it's unreal.

•   •   •

Right now a tramp called Rodney is rooting through yesterday's trash. I haven't seen him around in years, but now he's back, wearing a canvas hobo pack and a fisherman's vest. His hat with its dangling lures sits crooked on his head, and the fabric of his vest as well as his bare skin are olive colored with grime. His handlebar mustache has turned peppery white. Rodney's a Stanford graduate, also a former hippie. Fifteen years ago he was the most prominent bum in Calaveras Beach, but now he seems to have lost his mind. He keeps staring in my direction.

• • •

On good days I can levitate over the beach and the concrete stairs to the level of seagulls perching on sodium lamps along the strand. Sometimes I rise even higher than that, as high as a crow, and take in this whole suburb on the western edge of L.A. County—the swerve of seashore laced with surf, the railroad parallel to the beach, with its odor of dusty oleander and cinder bed; the parks, the school-yards, the cars, the acres of asphalt draping the town.

But most of the time I feel like an ordinary kid, physically solid and hale. Which is strange, because I was killed in 1984 by a boy named Tom Linden. He went down on manslaughter, and my death was apparently the result of an accident—teenagers in a car, no seat belts—though of course the cops and the courts got it wrong.

His mom is embittered by popular culture: She still thinks Tom was corrupted by *A Clockwork Orange*.

• • •

I go quiet sometimes. I seem to blink in and out, like a firefly. The periods of wakefulness can be long or short; I don't have any control over that. The periods of quiet are like a deep meditation or watching. When I get bored watching people on the beach or in the graveyard, I visit my parents on Nelson Street, or wander the town, or spend time in the library. Like a young yeshiva student I can sit for hours at the long library tables and pore over newspapers, magazines, novels, plays; books on astronomy, history, philosophy, religion, architecture, boating, or dog breeding. (I try to read only what strangers leave behind, to avoid lifting books off the shelves and spooking the staff.) The Calaveras Beach Western Branch Library is one of those ugly but functional government buildings put up in the deep Cold War, with broad picture windows hedged by junipers, and an official name or designation in iron letters bolted to the brick. It's not a major branch, and the books are outdated. But a modest life of the mind is better than nothing.

To me the most relevant document from the library is a yellowed page of the *Strand Bulletin*, which I managed to save from the recycling bin years ago by allowing it to fall behind a Xerox machine. The *Bulletin* is our local weekly, published every Thursday, and the item in question ran on May 24, 1984:

LOCAL BOY KILLED IN MYSTERY CRASH

Last Saturday, Eric Sperling, a sophomore from Calaveras High, was killed in an auto accident when the car in which he was riding rear-ended a truck on Vermont Avenue in downtown Los Angeles. The car had been stolen from the high school last October, and its driver, Tom Linden, a Calaveras freshman, has been charged with vehicular manslaughter as well as grand theft auto. The formerly green Chrysler was disguised with blue house-paint. It is not yet certain whether the victim knew he was riding in a stolen car, which made headlines last autumn and has baffled local authorities for months.

That's a good one. Of *course* I knew about the Chrysler! Teenagers are not complete idiots. Maybe the reporter wanted to spare my parents a rumor that I was involved in stealing the car. Very sensitive. The truth is, I had nothing to do with stealing it, but my parents in the end weren't spared the rumor, since it was all but printed right there on the front page of the *Bulletin*. Oh, well. I guess if the full truth got published in the paper my parents wouldn't even recognize me. They had enough trouble figuring out how a well-behaved boy like me could have died in a stolen car. The *Bulletin* doesn't even mention Rachel Cisneros, Rick Fisher, or a single gram of Colombian cocaine.

• • •

My dad is Jewish, my mom's Lutheran-German. I was raised Jewish because my dad's Orthodox parents had insisted on Hebrew school. So at the age of eleven or twelve I fell under the sway of Rabbi Gelanter, a large, restless bearded man with watery eyes and an insistent Brooklyn voice. Now I think of him as not just a rabbi, but also a member of his own upstart generation, because so many of the people he grew up with in the 1940s and '50s went on to become '60s revolutionaries and sometimes-flaky philosophical seekers. Gelanter had the same energy (and unruly looks) as a lot of his contemporaries; but instead of studying the I Ching or Zen Buddhism, he turned to his own tradition; to the Zohar, that massive work of Jewish mysticism. He was obsessed with the Zohar's three levels of the soul—*nefesh*, *ruach*, and *neshamah*—which he believed corresponded to measurable wavelengths, or levels of consciousness, in the brain. The Zohar says the *neshamah* belongs to God and goes to God when the body fails. The *ruach* is a kind of umbilical cord or conductor for the breath of life. And the *nefesh* is the human shape or spirit that wanders the world after death. Rabbi Gelanter thought these levels of the soul ruled certain functions of the mind. (*Nefesh* felt pleasure and pain, *ruach* chose between good and evil, *neshamah* engaged in philosophy and Torah study, and so on.) The point of making these distinctions was to understand what the self consisted of, and *nefesh* was just the tip of an island that plunged for miles into the sea.

As a kid, these ideas struck me as bizarre; I never took them seriously. But now I have a warm personal interest in anything the Zohar has to say. Last month I even stole one volume of it from the library. The full version runs to something like twenty-two volumes. *Zohar* in Hebrew means "splendor," and the books in general describe the vibrations or emanations of life and matter from a primal source. The idea is that a divine or hidden reality lies behind everyday experience. I still don't know whether I believe that or not, but this afterlife has given me some time to brood about the assumptions of my literal sixteen-year-old brain, and I have to admit that the idea of a deeper reality is, in a way, liberating. Everything we see emanates from something unseen. *Nefesh* emanates from *neshamah* as a flower blooms from a tree, or as the world emanates from God. A thirteenth-century rabbi wrote down these ideas in Spain, claiming they belonged to an ancient text that dated back more than a thousand years, to a time when Kabbalism and Christianity were both just little tributaries of the same wide, slow-flowing stream.

• • •

Tom Linden lives above a hardware store on the main road through Guerneville, a redwood-empire town in northern California. He's a blond house carpenter with tiny, smirking eyes and thickening flesh. His broad-windowed flat has spare old furniture and wooden floors painted thick dark brown. The fridge rattles; the floorboards moan. In the summer it's bloated and creaky, in the winter it's drafty and damp. Two years ago I traveled up there intending to haunt him, but I was timid about it, and he was too busy to notice anything as frail or evanescent as a ghost. His apartment was no more than a crash pad where he took care of basic needs between long days of construction work. He would get up at dawn and leave in his pickup for a series of sites around Sonoma County. He'd come home in the evening, dirty and tired and sometimes drunk from a visit to a bar.

When his girlfriend came over, they rented a video or just watched TV, and by the time I got up the nerve to creak a floorboard, or rap a wall, Tom was either involved with Jessie's body or stoned beyond consciousness on powerful Mendocino weed.

The *nefeshot* mentioned in the Zohar linger in the world to haunt old friends and weep over their own buried remains. The world itself is their purgatory. The troublesome part for me is that these spirits are supposed to finish wandering after no more than a year. (The Zohar is very specific about the time frame.) They strut and fret their hour until their corpses turn to dust, then take a bow and dissolve into the netherworld, like Mexican sugar skulls dropped into a glass of water.

What happens next, in the Zohar, is a "crowning," a spiritual accession to the throne. The *nefesh* gets crowned by the *ruach*, which then gets crowned by the *neshamah*, and they all rise to heaven together. (I picture them stacked, like those singing animals stacked on a donkey in the Grimms' fairy tale.) Even to a ghost, of course, this mysticism can read like organized nonsense. All I really know about my twilight condition is that haunting people is a kind of communication—the haunted person has to be ready for a visit. Tom wasn't. He was also on antidepressants. That felt somehow like cheating, and I went away from Guerneville thinking that modern pharmacology might put ghosts out of work.

• • •

Southern California has a lancing desert light that casts long shadows on the street, fading the glamour of Hollywood, the paint on hippie vans, and the pastel shop-signs in Calaveras Beach with the same uncalibrated lack of mercy. Banality rules around here; it scatters dreams like dust. By "dreams," I mean the real ones, the voices from the unconscious, as well as the idle ones people can buy. The last fifteen years have been so good to real estate prices in

Calaveras Beach that rich newcomers have razed the stuccoed houses of people I used to know and put up monstrous, bloated fantasies, with Roman arches and useless Greek columns—oversized, pompous things roofed in terra-cotta, painted pink or orange, and decorated with cute little gardens where you'd expect to find fairy lights or a couple of gnomes. Provincial palaces. McMansions. *Feh.* They'll be faded and horrible in fifteen years, and they're just another example of the retreat into illusion that outsiders associate with California—a strange affliction born of money, though not just of money.

My story has to do with this affliction. It takes place in a time when Calaveras Beach was still growing out of its old life as a funky, slow-paced ocean town. Gentrification, back then, looked like a function of President Reagan—it seemed wrapped up with his bubble economy and his dyed hair. But frivolity doesn't come and go with presidents. Most of the owners of these new mansions are Hollywood-style liberals, which doesn't surprise me at all, because why should self-deception pick sides?

• • •

Rodney peers at an empty Budweiser bottle and glances around in the fog. His face looks distorted. He limps away from me to a pier piling and sits against it, gazing across the beach like a grizzled sea captain. Gouts of fog drift between the pilings. The murmuring ocean rises, recedes. I wander over and sit beside him in the sand.

ii

The best place to start might be the handful of months when Tom and I were friends. Our families were friends, and my most important early memories of him are connected with his dad, Joe Linden, who died in a fishing accident in the spring of 1983. Joe Linden was an easygoing alcoholic who wore Hawaiian prints and had sharp blue eyes under sagging lids. I liked him well enough, but Tom flowed with an idealistic anger toward everything he represented. "My dad would be all right if he'd just quit *lying* to himself," he used to say.

My mom had the Lindens over for lunch every Saturday in the summer of 1983 because Greta Linden suffered brutal mood swings in the wake of her husband's death. Greta was German, like my mom. She could be merry with piping laughter or sad-voiced and bleak. Her pink nose had a cauliflower shape, her eyes were small; the flesh of her fingers overflowed her wedding ring. She had short, thin blond hair, and bracelets that tinkled on her heavy wrists.

Tom was about to start as a freshman at Calaveras High, where I would be a sophomore, and I guess our parents thought I could be a surrogate older brother for him, a moral chaperon or a guide. That's funny to think about now, because Tom's career as a delinquent started right under my nose. I enabled him. At fifteen and sixteen I was lanky and bookish, with a bird's-nest shag of wavy black hair—a gawky young shlemiel who believed almost everything anybody said. Tom found me easy to convince. But how was I supposed to know any better? Until then we'd been like cousins, distant friends with no particular reason to avoid each other, and even after a weird incident with an axe, I never thought he would kill me.

At first we played basketball on Saturdays at Calaveras High. Tom wound up losing so often on those broken courts he should have gotten used to it, but he would still curse and turn red and nearly pop a neck vein every time he fell behind.

After a month of basketball, he declared himself sick of sports, and one Saturday we hung around the so-called Swamp, which was a patch of eucalyptus trees and mud just downhill from the school. The Swamp lay hidden from the street behind the campus of a remedial school called Pacific Shores. (The kids who misbehaved or failed at Calaveras High moved literally down, to Swamp-level, where they finished their high-school careers in two long puce-painted bungalows.) Tom climbed a eucalyptus next to one of the bungalows with an eager, monkeylike energy: I watched him inch along a heavy branch until it bent and dropped him on the flat gravel roof. He looked like an average California kid, sockless and skeptical, with short, very light blond hair and blond eyebrows.

The branch sprang up behind him, waving its leaves. He walked a few steps to pick up some heavy tool.

"Hey look. Somebody left an axe up here," he said.

"Great."

It was a sway-handled firewood axe with a rusty blade. Tom flipped it off the building and it wheeled once before thunking, blade-first, into the soil. He clambered down to retrieve it.

"Blade's still sharp," he said.

"It couldn't have been up there long."

"Why not? There's rust on it."

"But no one at Shores could have left it there. It's like leaving a gun around."

"Maybe one of the kids was hiding it," he said. "Maybe someone got killed and the murderer threw it up on the roof." He scratched at the rust. "Maybe this is *blood*," he said with a squint-eyed smile.

"Maybe."

Tom swung the axe at a eucalyptus tree, leaving a fibrous green wound. "Come on!" He started hacking weeds as he stomped off in the direction of a nearby church.

I followed him to a zigzag fence separating the Swamp from the church parking lot. He stopped at a peppercorn tree that grew sideways from a crook in the fence, looking for light under a clump of eucalyptus. He tapped the tree with the heavy axe head.

"You think it belongs to the church?" he said.

"What do you mean?"

" 'Cause of where it's growing?"

The peppercorn grew on the Swamp side, but leaned toward the church. I cleared my throat.

"I'd say it's a Swamp tree."

"Really?"

"Sure. In court, I don't think the church would have a case." I shrugged. "If they'd made that fence straight, it might be their tree, but—not with a crooked fence like that."

"In court." I could see him trying to think like a lawyer. "Is that how it works? Just wherever you build your fence?"

"I don't see how else it would work."

Tom nodded sagely. Then he hacked into the tree at waist level, raining peppercorns onto our heads. The tree was gnarled and grey, ant-ridden, with small pale leaves. Its branches mingled with the surrounding trees. I felt nervous. At fifteen I had an over-developed sense of responsibility; everything I did came freighted with grave consequences. At the same time—not exactly by accident—I was more than happy to let other kids misbehave on my behalf. If Tom wanted to do interesting things, I was willing to watch.

He chopped, hard, with a concentrated rage. After a minute, I felt remorse.

"What are you *doing?*"

"What does it look like?"

"You can't just cut down that tree."

"Why not?"

"It's not yours! Stop it."

"You said it was a Swamp tree," he said.

"I said it was a Swamp tree but that doesn't mean 'Maybe you should cut it down.' "

"I don't need your *permission.*"

He turned red as he chopped. Each hack exposed more greenish flesh. I started to get mad. Finally I grabbed the axe with both hands. "Stop it."

"Let go," he said.

"Stop cutting the tree."

"Let *go.*" He wrenched the axe from my hands. His eyes looked bright and hot. "How come you gotta interfere? You don't care about this tree."

"I'm just saying it's wrong."

"Why is it wrong? Who says?"

"Whaddayou mean, who says? Everyone just knows it's wrong."

"Oh, yeah?" Tom said, with a challenging gleam in his eye that I actually admired. "Hah."

Now I hesitated. The trunk was already frayed; pale pulp stood out like hair. If I was honest, I had to admit that the only reason I wanted him to stop hacking the tree was that I wanted him to stop hacking the tree. What else could I say? No appeal to conventional rules would have swayed him. His face was wild. Not only had he made me feel like a wimp, overworried about what everyone thought—and the idea of throwing caution to the wind like Tom made me shake with excitement and fear—he also looked ready to swing the blade at my chest.

I stepped back. Tom went on chopping. When the tree came loose, he hollered, *"Look out!"* and covered his head like a soldier who's thrown a grenade. But nothing happened. The other trees sagged, holding the peppercorn up by its branches.

"Nice one," I said.

Until that moment, the church lot had been empty; now a long school bus pulled in from the road and parked squarely across from where we stood. Noisy kids watched us from the windows. Tom whispered, "Piss!" and let the axe slip from his fingers. He started down the hill, but I lingered long enough to see a woman step out of the bus and give me a quizzical look. By then a crowd of kids had spilled into the lot. I ran, and found Tom behind a Shores bungalow, sitting with his arms around his knees. Red peppercorns stuck to his hair, dry and faded, like tiny desiccated cherries.

"You get caught?" he said.

"Some teacher saw me."

"We should wait here."

I caught my breath and sat. We didn't have to wait long because Harold Ivins appeared at the bungalow corner, holding the axe. Harold was a full-fledged delinquent who worked as a church counselor to fulfill some community-service element of his probation from juvenile hall. He had buzzed hair the color of wheat stubble and a toothy, leering grin. He should have graduated from Calaveras High in the spring, but he'd been expelled the year before for bad grades, and for doing doughnuts on school grounds in his pickup. Now he went to Pacific Shores.

"Hey, guys," he said.

Tom jumped to his feet and tried to run. Harold stopped him by holding the sharp edge of the axe close to his arm. "Ta-a-ake it easy there, faggot," he said in a cheerful, almost familiar voice.

"Where'd *you* come from?" Tom asked.

Harold nodded at the bus. "We're all back from a nice day on the beach," he said. "Took the kids boogie boarding."

"Well," said Tom. "We were just sitting here."

"Oh yeah? Not chopping trees?"

Tom shook his head.

"We saw you from the bus, faggot." He put a strange emphasis on this word. "You and your goony friend."

"Whatever. We weren't doing anything."

Harold smiled, but rounded his eyes so they bulged from his head. At eighteen, Harold looked to us like a mature man, with real hair on his forearms and some blond moss on his chin. His skin had grown tanned and craggy where ours was still callow and smooth. His brutal moods had an adult's authority, which was terrifying. He grabbed Tom's arm and squeezed. "Don't act wise," he snapped, and in a quick smooth motion with one corner of the blade he nicked Tom between the eyes, just on the bridge of his nose. Tom jerked his head back. A bright bead of blood stood out.

"Damn," he breathed.

"You cut down a good tree over there—property of Trinity Methodist Church. I saw it, and so did Miss Tucker. You can't do that around here, okay? Especially not in front of the kids."

Tom nodded. I did, too, although Harold was technically on my side. He was succeeding where I had just failed. Still, I hated him. I resented the way he used his church-counselor job to order people around. The bead of blood ran down one side of Tom's nose.

"It's not the church's tree," I said.

Harold turned his face, with bulging eyes, as if he hadn't quite noticed me before.

"What did you say?"

"It's on the Swamp side of the fence."

His cheeks flushed. He twisted his head toward the peppercorn. Our angle wasn't good, so he said, "Come on," with a wave of the axe. In full view—again—of the kids, who were huddled like goats in the lot, we had a good look at that stump. Harold breathed heavily while he made up his mind. Cogitation, for him, was hard work.

"Okay," he concluded. "Now listen. I don't give a flying *fuck* whose tree this is. But I see it like this. If I *ever* find *either one* of you guys around here again, I'm gonna kick both of your asses to Inglewood. Got it? Cutting a tree is, like, *vandalism*. It sets a bad example for the kids." He stared again; we nodded. "And I don't want anyone setting a bad example for the kids while I'm on this job, because I gotta finish summer out here before I'm done with probation. And I don't want any of you little faggots trying to screw things up. Understand?"

We must have indicated that we did. Harold let Tom go.

"Now get out of here."

We slipped through a gap in the fence and stopped on the Calaveras High running track. I looked at Tom's face. "You should wash that off." We climbed the bleachers on the far edge of the field, to where the campus proper started, and found a water fountain against one of the school buildings.

"How do you know Harold?" I asked.

"I've just seen him around."

"How come he calls you faggot?"

"It's just what he says."

"He doesn't call me that."

"What does he call you?"

"I don't know, he doesn't know what to call me. He ignores me most of the time."

Tom had been splashing water on his face. He straightened up, looking uncomfortable with this conversation. "Well, what do you wanna do? Our moms are still back at your place."

"Yeah."

"Let's go to Mr. B's."

"All right."

This idea seemed to animate him. We started walking across the pavement, and he said, "Maybe we can steal a *Playboy*."

Was he serious? Theft was wrong, in my opinion. I felt scared and a little surprised.

"What for?" I said.

"What *for*," he scolded. "Jesus."

I chuckled, trying to seem casual. But then I stopped walking. He turned and squinted.

"Didn't you ever steal a *Playboy* before?"

"No."

"Well, come on, then. I'll show you how. I've done it a bunch of times."

"Isn't it against the law? I mean, not just store rules, but like—"

"Of *course* it's against the law! Jesus Christ! But look: It's against the law for us to buy it, too. It's against the law for us to *read* it until we're eighteen. So how are we supposed to see *Playboy* unless we steal it?"

"I—" His logic was hard to argue down. "I don't know."

"So then come on."

Mr. B's stood on the corner of an intersection with Artesia Boulevard, about a block from school. In our lifetimes the store had never seen a fresh coat of paint. Bleeding across a crown of corrugated Fiberglas was a majestic, ancient-looking plastic initial—

Mr. *B*'s

—and the owner, Dave Bartholomew, sat massively behind his counter in mismatched plaid. His tiny feminine mouth was nested between drooping jowls, and when you walked in his weak eyes moved suspiciously from a tiny TV to the door. The place was crowded with limpid bottles of liquor as well as cigars, chaw twists, humidors, pipes, Swisher Sweets, Kentucky cheroots, and snuff. It had the odor of stale tobacco and maybe spilled beer. Parent groups and administrators had made it their business to close him down, but Bartholomew owned the tiny strip mall he part-occupied, so their activism led to nothing but a slowly tightening series of rules on us. We went in anyway. He had things teenagers liked—soft drinks, candy, an aging video game—but we could never tell if Mr. B was our friend, because he looked so much like one of those Ralph Steadman cartoons of a cop or a conventioneer in *Fear and Loathing in Las Vegas* (one of our favorite books).

The store's gone now, of course. For six or seven years it's been a 7-Eleven. But it was an important place for us as kids, and Tom knew about it from an early age because his dad was a regular customer.

The first thing we noticed—or realized, since I guess we'd noticed it before—was that Mr. B kept his pornography in a rack behind the counter. "What do we do?" I whispered.

Tom said, "Just watch. Don't say anything."

He stepped up to the counter and asked Bartholomew to change a dollar. Then he went back to the video game. Mr. B kept an eye on our backs while Tom played. Did he recognize us? He should have, since we'd been there often enough with Joe Linden. Tom's dad was the first grown-up to introduce either of us to certain masculine rites, like shopping for booze, and looking back now I can see how many con-man qualities Tom had absorbed from him. They were both shysters. Mr. Linden was a real-estate agent who made a sizable second income through certain shady side deals. Three months earlier, he'd embarrassed himself pretty badly in front of us by giving a sales pitch to Mr. B about time-share condos that the old man must have heard twice before. I remembered Mr. Linden leaning on the counter with one elbow—long-faced, all business—to pass along what was meant to be a select morsel of investment advice. "Tourist condos. Time-share deals," he said. "Right down on the beach close to Mazatlán. Going for a steal right now."

"No—kiddin'."

"I'm showing some guys around after our fishing trip this year. These surfside deals are the next frontier in tourism."

No one knew what "the next frontier in tourism" meant, but it was the sort of thing you heard from Mr. Linden all the time. During the seventies he'd sold my parents megavitamins; yellowish powders scooped from cardboard tubs to make supernutritious milk shakes. I remember my parents sitting at the table with milky mustaches, reacting politely to the flavor of the drinks while Mr. Linden went on about his increased alertness and energy level.

"Hey, Dad," Tom said in a sharp voice. "You *told* him about this already. He's not interested."

Mr. Linden raised his eyebrows, like Dean Martin caught in a camera flash.

"Did I?" he said.

Mr. B stared. "I think you did."

"Well—" For a terrible moment, his investment pitch lay exposed as a cheap con. But Mr. Linden found a way to recover. "I guess I'm just so worked up about this deal I can't contain myself!"

Bartholomew slid the brown-bagged bottle in his customer's direction.

"Let me know how it goes."

"You bet I will."

His cheerful assurances were like dust. Mr. Linden must have sensed this about himself. On some level, he must have known that he was on a downhill slide. No one ever learned whether Mexican beach resorts were the next frontier in tourism because he was killed two weeks later by falling from his fishing boat and knocking his head on the propeller. The only person to see it happen was my dad, who was sitting a few yards away in a canvas chair. When they found his body, with a floodlight, Mr. Linden was already dead from the gash in his skull, floating in a cloud of blood.

Anyway, while Tom banged on the video game, he whispered: "Is he still watching?"

"Yeah."

"Go buy something."

"Why?"

"Just do it. How much money do you have?"

"Like fifty cents."

"Go buy something. As a distraction."

"What are you gonna do?" I kept my frantic voice to a whisper. "All his magazines are behind the counter."

"Go buy a Snickers." He slapped the video game again as if he'd lost his turn, which he hadn't. Then, with the air of someone who couldn't wait all day for other people to sort out their bullshit, he hurried down the tobacco aisle.

At first I just stood there. I didn't like being ordered around. I wandered over to the brass candy rack and picked out a Kit Kat. Mr. B's counter was half as long as the rear of the store, and the *Playboys* sat next to a Skoal display on a shelf behind him. The shelf was bookended by a tall rack of chips. Tom rustled through the chips for a while and came to the register with a package of Frito's. Bartholomew glared. He parted with his change more slowly than usual.

"Whaddayou got in your pocket?" he asked Tom.

"Me? Nothing."

"Lemme see."

"See what?"

"Turn your pockets inside out."

Tom whined, "What the *fuck?*", but did as he was told. Bartholomew watched us both with wasted eyes.

"Okay," he said, and we left.

The sun flaring off the lot outside was deadening; the whole town felt bleak under the relentless summer heat. "Well?" I said, and Tom pulled a can of Skoal from the waistband of his shorts.

"*Chewing* tobacco?" I said. "Big deal."

Then he produced a folded-over *Playboy*.

"How'd you do that!" I cried. "I was watching! Those magazines weren't close enough to the chip rack."

"Yeah, but he keeps a couple for himself right by the Skoal."

I watched him for a second, eyes still round with astonishment.

"That's gross!"

"I know." He opened the can and stuffed a pinch of the moist black stuff into his cheek.

"Wan' thome?"

"Sure."

So we went back to the Swamp and flipped through *Playboy* while my blood ran cold from the nicotine. The bitter poisonous taste of tobacco made my head spin; the glossy pictures aroused me. I almost passed out. But I must have held my own through this whole rite of passage, because Tom never seemed to notice any lapse in form. Dipping Skoal took the kind of masochistic self-denial that would mark almost everything I tried, from schoolwork to delinquency. It was something I learned in Hebrew school. Like a lot of good kids, I took selflessness to a fanatic extreme.

In those days I was just growing out of shlemielhood, out of a fierce and boyish devotion to rules. Rabbi Gelanter used to call Judaism the oldest world tradition founded on the "principle of freedom," but I was skeptical. Six hundred and thirteen commandments listed in the Books of Moses—some of them forbidding us cheeseburgers—and our rabbi argues that the legend of freedom from Egypt is the metaphorical basis for the whole religion. Obeying those rules, he said, was how Jews *became* free, and I guess it made sense if you took the laws as a survival guide for the ancient desert. But in California we didn't have to worry about survival; "freedom" had a different meaning. We wanted the kind of freedom that impresses every American kid—a kinetic, undirected individual liberty, defiant but lively. Freedom from what? Didn't matter. Our country's founding rhetoric of freedom from kings and taxes had altered, fermented, but never died, and Americans ever since the Revolution had been rolling west to be free of Old World stodginess, Eastern class-consciousness, urban congestion, bad wages, slavery, poverty, rotten weather. California was the far edge of the frontier, host to the gold rush, breeding ground for hippie culture, the start of the Pacific Ocean. Freedom was the whole point of our state as well as our nation. And from the end of our pier you could stand like one of Melville's sentinels and look even further west, across a salt expanse that covered the barnacled cities of aircraft carriers lying only half-ruined on the ocean floor—or glowing fish, or island-spewing volcanic vents—things you heard about but couldn't quite believe. You imagined how it might feel to sail to Australia with the wind in your face, and ocean mist stinging your eyes; you wondered about tidal waves, the Marianas Trench, or the lost continent of Atlantis (different ocean, but never mind)—and then, as an overwhelmed fifteen-year-old, you mounted your rusty ten-speed and rode home in time for dinner.

iv

School started two weeks later, and Tom joined the sea of faces in our sunlit, banging locker halls. He rolled to campus on a skateboard and walked anonymously to class with his backpack slung from both shoulders and his blond hair freshly trimmed. He wore ordinary Izod shirts and leather Topsiders. If it weren't for the unpleasant look on his face he could have run for student government.

Our campus was (and still is) a sprawling, strangely military village of sand-colored stucco and chalky white brick that processed maybe two thousand students a year—mostly placid suburban kids whose bright-eyed personalities and sun-bleached hair mirrored the self-contented quaintness of our beachfront shops. The core group of Future Leaders wore polo shirts and plaid Bermudas, were all good-looking, had fine social skills, and seemed to pass judgment in their manner, in the very narrowness of their social radar, on the students outside their cliques. Yuppies-in-training. Full of bland lassitude and money ambition. The rest of us hated them. They were snobbish, conformist, shallow, and cute. They were good at sports and had sex lives. They weren't stupid, but they also weren't too smart.

My friends and I ate lunch by the flagpole on a patch of grass in the middle of campus, quiet and unexciting. For Tom we must have been the wrong group to be seen with, because he would turn out to be very sensitive about his image. Only now, thinking back, do I realize how true this is. Tom would never admit to such a feminine weakness, but vanity was his driving force.

My two closest friends were both named Doug. Doug Pease had brownish frog lips on a soft face, a puff of curly hair, and clear blue eyes. His dad was an aerospace engineer (like mine), and the time he spent in front of his computer was advertised by the turned-milk color of his skin. My other friend, Doug Swillinger, was unusually tall, with one blind stray eye and a hunchback he disguised under loud plaid coats. At the end of the summer he had found a job at a local art-house called the Bijou, as assistant projectionist, which made him a kind of Quasimodo of the projection room. I've never met anyone as deeply unusual as Doug Swillinger. At least some of his strangeness was a side effect of a heart disease that would kill him before he was twenty. I think an early awareness of death burned away the foolishness that possessed the rest of us, so Doug was odd, a sexless presence with straight dark hair dangling in his eyes—subtle and mordant and removed from the Calaveras cult of the body.

Ten years ago I watched Doug's coffin go into the dirt behind the First Presbyterian Church, only a couple of miles from my grave at the Temple Beth-El Shalom. But I never see him haunting the sidewalks or lingering on the beach by the pier. It's odd. Sometimes I wonder what happened to him. Death turns out to be a lonely, solitary condition. That sounds like a cliché, I know, but for someone in my position it comes as kind of a surprise. The fact that I never see *anyone* around—not Doug, not Joe Linden, not a single perished soul—makes me worry that the real ghosts have found a better place to congregate.

In the first week of school, Tom sat with us for the duration of a ham sandwich and studied a girl named Rachel, who hung out with a crowd of what Doug Pease called "stoners," on a low cinder-block wall. They weren't really stoners. They were a loose, eclectic band made up of the drug-taking fringes of various other cliques. They resisted the conservative tone of Calaveras Beach with a sixties-descended alternative cool. There were honor students, musicians, surfers, and would-be politicians. Rachel, their exotic queen, was a surfer with a shameless gypsy smile. She was part Filipina and part Mexican, with short full lips and sloe eyes hidden under tousled hair. On the day Tom noticed her she was flirting with some boy, throwing out sharp peals of laughter and curling up her sandaled brown toes.

"That's Rachel Cisneros," I told him. "She's a sophomore."

Tom squinted and nodded cannily. He pretended not to care, although Rachel, for a time, would become his entire world.

Soon he got up to leave.

"See you," he said.

"Bye."

Tom was even more alienated at Calaveras High than I expected. He didn't seem to have any friends from middle school. One reason may have been that the Lindens lived in a gated community called Windsor Gardens. Most of us had been raised on broken-asphalt streets and noisy sidewalks, but Tom belonged to a quiet colony of housing units painted nice pastel colors and shaded by imported palm trees. Behind an imposing pair of *faux*-elegant iron gates an air of exclusiveness was maintained by pristine frog ponds and a sore lack of parking. Gated communities were ancestors to the current fashion for monster homes, but in spite of the elegant sheen all the adults seemed to understand that Windsor Gardens amounted to nothing more than a glorified apartment complex. Even my parents' shabby stucco bungalow, with its sagging deck overlooking a weed-grown driveway, was a stronger foothold on the slopes of wealth than the Lindens' fancy condo.

I don't mean Tom was deprived, or somehow labeled as a "gated-community boy." I just mean he had the seclusion of money without the privileges. Also—I forget this sometimes—Tom was adopted. He looked like, but wasn't, the Lindens' biological son. The only clue to his origins was a note in his adoption file: "Burbank, California." But Tom never pursued it; he never wondered about his real parents, and as far as I know, he never tried to find them.

Anyway, one morning in September our school held a sex-ed assembly in the auditorium. We lined up under a sprawling cypress tree, in two lines—one for boys and one for girls. Tom stood by himself, a few spaces back from the Dougs and me. I remember him stealing secret glances at girls. The day was bright and cold, so a lot of them wore zippered cotton sweatshirts, formless hooded garments with almost nothing underneath, exposing necklaces on collarbones, wedges of beautiful skin, and sometimes even a bra strap caught on the knob of a shoulder. Rachel was there, chewing her thumbnail. Other girls had on Guess jeans, light ski wear, or windbreakers. They stood in clusters, *discussing*, darting their bright quick eyes.

Just behind Tom stood three friends of Harold Ivins's: Jeremy, Ryker, and Drew. The biggest, Ryker, had thin blond hair on top of a big, sloping frame. His eyes were narrow and sleepy and he looked like Barney Rubble. After a few minutes, Doug Pease said, "Hey. Those guys are picking on Tom," and I looked over. Tom touched his arm tenderly with one hand, scowling. Ryker and Drew harassed him in low voices, which we could just make out.

"It doesn't matter where I heard it, putz."

"Are you a faggot?"

"No."

"Say you are."

"No."

They punched him in the arm.

"Admit it."

"No."

These were large kids. Their muscles bulged and they knew where to hit.

"Say you are."

"No."

Each punch made a hard dull smack. They knuckled him right on the bone.

"Just say you are and we'll quit hitting you."

"No."

Girls watched the commotion with lightly wrinkled foreheads. Two teachers, undevoted to discipline, waited by the door for orders to let us in. They didn't intervene. Harold's friends tried to be careful, too: Ryker raised his head with a blank and innocent expression, watched until all teachers were distracted, then grabbed Tom's arm and gave it quick sharp blows so muted and surreptitious I only saw his shoulders jerk.

"How come they're doing that?" Doug Pease said.

"Because they're assholes?"

"Oh."

When the teachers opened the auditorium, we filed in. Boys and girls were segregated by the center aisle, and Tom sat with us. Harold's friends leered in our direction as if we were all at risk of being gay. They gave up torturing Tom in favor of trying to sit as close as possible to the screen and rolling spit wads.

"What was that about?" I said.

"Nothing."

"They were calling you 'faggot' again. Just like Harold was."

"So?"

"So what's it about?"

"Ask *them*, man. I don't fucking know. They've been doing it since last year."

"At Granger?" Our middle school. "What happened?"

Tom shook his head. "It's really stupid."

I waited.

"You really want to hear it?"

"Of course."

"Well, in the hall one time, they passed me and tried to hit me? Just like they hit everybody. So I tried to hit Jeremy back. But I clenched my hand too late and accidentally grabbed his ass."

"You're kidding."

He shrugged. "That's what happened. I tried to tell them it was an accident, but they wouldn't listen. They're all, 'Yeah, right, like you didn't mean to grab his ass.' "

"That sucks, Tom. They're idiots."

The story sounded untrue, or half-true. But I felt sorry for him. Granger Middle School was like a jail, all brown-painted banks of lockers and acres of chain-link fence. For boys the dominant school-yard questions were *Who's a faggot?* and *Who's a wimp?* I was glad to get out of there.

In the next few weeks, Tom acted nervous and edgy during lunch. Instead of eating with us, he wandered around campus and sat by himself in the middle of a baseball field or in the juniper bushes next to the gym. From a distance I sometimes noticed him struggling in the quad with Harold's friends. They liked to grab his backpack, slug his arm, and keep slugging until he disentangled his elbows from the straps and ran away, leaving his pack in their hands. Normally they just kicked it across the yard, for Tom to find later, but sometimes

Ryker flung the backpack onto the roof of a locker hall, or dangled it from a tree.

The anguish must have been huge. I can only guess what he was going through. Not only was his father dead, not only was he new at school, but Harold's buddies wouldn't even let him suffer in peace. Tom had nothing to stand on, socially—no profile of his own, no clear group of friends—and when I look back in the silence of some foggy morning like this, in a compassionate mood, I think the torture he suffered in his first months of ninth grade is what taught him how to hate.

V

In early October, the Bijou put *A Clockwork Orange* on the marquee for a limited run. Doug Swillinger promised to get us in for free. He also invited Tom, and when Mrs. Linden learned her son had been invited to a movie, she took the humiliating step of inviting everyone over for dinner. Soon our two mothers had stirred up so much excitement over "Tom's new friends" that on a Friday evening we had no choice but to show up at the Lindens' white-trimmed yellow unit in Windsor Gardens for lasagna. Greta had prepared a three-course meal. She moved around the brilliant kitchen with a glass of wine, wearing a lime green pantsuit and addressing us all as "you boys."

"Would you boys like a soda?" she asked us. "Tom, why don't you get out some plates for your friends. We'll have nachos in a moment."

Tom stalked into the kitchen and brought out a stack of plates. Doug Swillinger sat on one end of the couch. He picked up a large decorative crystal egg from an end table and turned it curiously in his hand.

The living room had a Dri-Erase quality, with deep ivory carpet on the floor and hazy maritime scenes on the walls. Mr. Linden's presence still dominated: There was a gleaming stuffed marlin mounted over the fireplace, and a smoked-glass liquor cabinet beside the TV. I wondered about his accident while we waited on the couch. What could have been going through his head? It was hard to imagine anyone less prepared for death than Joe Linden on the deck of a fishing boat. The way my dad described it, the sun had slipped under the edge of the water, and things were dusky and vague beyond the lights of the deck. Mr. Linden had wandered to the railing, alone, with a drink. Was he just drunk and melancholy from the sunset? Careless and exhausted? In any way suicidal? Maybe there was some problem with his time-share condos in Mazatlán, or maybe he was just thinking about his largest catch of the day, a six-foot barracuda drawn up on a bottom-trolling line, photographed by my dad with its eyes exploded and its guts looped out from the rapid decompression, still twisting on the hook with an expression of final surprise.

"Nachos," sang Mrs. Linden.

"Wow. Thanks."

We gathered around the pile of food. Mrs. Linden sipped her wine. She asked us about school in a well-mannered way that seemed to aggravate Tom. He chewed with his eyelids lowered, quietly.

"So what are you boys gonna see?" she asked.

"*A Clockwork Orange*," said Doug Swillinger.

"What does that mean?"

Doug explained that it was Cockney slang. "You say, 'That's queer as a clockwork orange.' "

"It's not pornographic, is it?"

"No, no."

After the nacho course we had lasagna and more Diet Coke.

Mrs. Linden was a good cook, and not a bad conversationalist. To us she seemed perfectly kind. Tom didn't respect her, though, and I think one reason had to do with Greta's hopelessly unhip Germanness, her awkward Old World accommodations to the pop desert of southern California. She looked ordinary enough for Braunschweig, her hometown, but she had the wrong shape for a beach city, and maybe to mitigate the foreignness of her natural heft she listened to soft rock, wore sweatsuits, and jogged. Even her accent had a slangy California edge. Tom thought these were the wrong accommodations. He would have preferred a mom who listened to Dvořák and spoke only Latvian to one who tried so embarrassingly to fit in.

After lasagna we piled into Mrs. Linden's car and rode to the Bijou. We bought popcorn and found a place to sit. *A Clockwork Orange* was still taboo for us; we knew it only by name and reputation, and we liked the way its reputation seemed to violate the comfortable sunniness of Calaveras Beach. Tom's eyes glittered in the dark and he seemed to drink in Alex's grim sense of humor and pitiless voice while the rest of us cracked jokes and chewed on greasy popcorn. We watched the movie through to the cynical final scene—"I'd been cured all right"— with strains of Beethoven's Ninth playing over an operatic, slow-motion fuck. After the lights came on, Tom said, "That was a *cool* movie," and the rest of us nodded.

Nothing in that movie really mirrors my death, but *A Clockwork Orange* left a deep mark on Tom. Alex and his droogs in the movie like to steal cars, and they live in a Soviet-style apartment block where nothing blooms or thrives—basically a dark cartoon of Windsor Gardens. During a wild joy ride one night, they rape and kill a woman in her house. Alex gets arrested, and a team of government scientists and sadistic cops condition him to feel sick at his own violent impulses using cruel Pavlovian methods. Maybe this taming of a wild boy flattered some prejudice in Tom about how the civilized world behaved, or maybe he was just seduced by the violence; in any case, he tacked a *Clockwork Orange* poster to his bedroom wall, after we saw the movie, and his mom hated it. The image of Alex holding a knife out at the viewer—almost into Tom's bedroom—became the flash point for a long mother-son struggle. They bickered about it, but Tom was stubborn. The poster stayed up.

In the weeks after my funeral, Greta suffered a huge upwelling of confusion and remorse over how she'd managed Tom in the wake of her husband's death, and she felt, no less than my mom or dad, the fundamental sense of failure all parents must suffer when a child slips away from their protection. Their friendship never caved in, but for a long time the weight of feeling between my parents and Greta was more than the usual rituals of white wine and weekend lunches could support, and Greta weathered a personal hell she had done nothing deliberate to deserve.

The antidote to this hell was activism. Greta started with small-time slide shows in front of school boards and PTAs, but now she runs a powerful watchdog organization based in Beverly Hills, with offices all around the country. Her network of fax machines emit press releases every time a movie comes out that crosses some threshold of obscenity or violence. Certain movies should be banned, say the releases. Greta herself showers politicians with E-mail and phone calls to ban them. Her success has been limited, but not too limited. It worries some free-speech types; and since my "accident" is still the hidden source of her zealotry, I figure I should come up with some kind of formal opinion.

I don't want to be glib, though. Imagine the headlines if I ever got through to a newspaper: MURDER VICTIM SAYS LAY OFF HORROR FLICKS. I know even better than Greta what kind of influence that movie had over Tom, and even if I can't honestly blame Stanley Kubrick for my death, I also have to wonder why *A Clockwork Orange* bit so hard into my murderer's brain. He was primed for it, like a lump of clay. What made him so malleable? "Violent movies appeal to their primitive instincts," Greta explains in her presentations, with a guttural German roll in the *r*. "They act out the explosive fantasies of all children before they grow up and become civilized. Adolescence is a passionate, primitive time of life, and as they grow up we must teach our children to be responsible, not encourage them to revert to savage animal behavior."

True, Greta! Or anyway, true as far as it goes. But isn't there another level? I mean, questions of character come into it, too. Character and upbringing. In English class that September I read something by Emerson that seemed to slip right under the eyes of the other kids, something I haven't forgotten. Emerson wrote, "High be his heart, faithful his will, clear his sight, that he may in good earnest be doctrine, society, law, to himself, that a simple purpose may be to him as strong as iron necessity is to others!" O God, *yes!* I thought when I first read that passage. Doctrine, society, law! It was an anti-shlemiel's manifesto. As a mopey kid I had urges and hopes in me that were fierce but embarrassing, and I wanted to harness them to become a self-motivated, yet wise, master of my own destiny.

The result was near-total paralysis. I couldn't trust myself to do anything. In fact, my craving for that kind of autonomy made me susceptible, for a while, to Tom, because I thought his showy independence was the whole idea. There's no lack of people around who say they're for "individualism," and Tom was one of them. He must have craved the real thing even more than I did. His moods after Mr. Linden's death slipped from gloom to enthusiasm in ungovernable, almost lunar cycles, so he needed independence and self-control at least as much as I wanted a way out of my own crippling hesitation. But in the end he wasn't curious enough to achieve it. I guess that's a roundabout way to explain why he was so impressionable. No matter how independent Tom acted, no matter how tough he seemed, the weakness of his mind and the brute force of his emotions meant he still had to go wherever the winds were gusting, and in high school they gusted toward delinquency. So it shouldn't be a huge surprise, Greta, that his career as a criminal was kindled by *A Clockwork Orange*, or that the first thing he did, after our trip to the Bijou, was put acid in Mr. Cantwell's coffee.

part two

vi

Surfers float in the water; the fog has lifted. It should be a hot summer day. Rodney scowls into the distance with drilling, bushy-browed eyes. Mexican fishermen on the pier have retreated to their cars, lugging heavy buckets and rods, and groups of teenagers have come down here with towels to claim a place on the sand. They're thin-bodied boys and willowy girls, probably students from Calaveras High. The local cheekbones and flat California voices haven't changed much in ten or fifteen years, although school itself must be an edgier experience, because it was rare in my generation for a suburban kid to get killed by a classmate. In that sense, at least, I was a pioneer. Now—since last April—getting shot in school is just one of those everyday freak risks for a teenager, like getting hit by lightning, and the current principal at Calaveras High has already fenced off the center of campus with ugly chain-link gates. The students live almost like a population at war, under the sickening shadow of Columbine.

Some of these kids probably remember Mr. Cantwell. Until he retired a couple of years ago, Cantwell taught driver training as well as freshman English, so every student at school had to meet him. He was a character on campus in spite of himself. He would lecture, cross-legged, from his aluminum stool, then suddenly stand and walk to the door, glance outside, frown, find and lose again his stained mug of coffee, marking his suit all the while with patches of chalk from his hands. He wore the same brown suit to class every day and changed only the pattern of his loosely knotted tie. His harried face sank in at the cheeks; his hair was receding. And his voice quacked. When kids imitated Mr. Cantwell, they sounded like Daffy Duck.

But his eccentricity didn't spring from a deep imagination. It was just the jitteriness of a career bureaucrat, a public-school apparatchik whose passionate goal was to raise our scores on the state's standardized reading exam. Mr. Cantwell believed that a high school's mission was to prepare students for the workplace. Instead of devoting himself to the art of teaching us to read, and to the corollary art of teaching us to think, he reduced a handful of poems and novels and plays to buckets of trivia we would need for the test.

Tom sat next to a Korean kid named Chuan in Mr. Cantwell's English class. One morning Chuan slipped a small square of paper onto his desk.

"What's this?" Tom asked.

"Put that in Mr. Cantwell's mug."

"What? How come?"

"It's a sweetener."

"What do you mean?"

"It's like Nutrasweet. Quick, before he gets here."

This was Period Two, before the bell. Most of the other kids were sleepily unfolding notebooks and opening bags. Jeremy watched from two rows away. Chuan—almost everyone knew—was enemies with Mr. Cantwell by descent. His drug-dealing older brothers had hated him. He carried acid and marijuana to school in his backpack, and he was plump, with large lidded eyes and a pouting face.

"This isn't Nutrasweet," Tom said.

"Whatever."

"What is it?"

"Just put it in. Hurry."

"I think this is LSD."

"Whatever. *Hurry.*"

Tom's eyebrows went up and he laughed.

"You better hurry," said Chuan.

"You do it."

"You're closer."

"Just *do* it, you putz," Jeremy Salter said from the other row, in his deep decisive voice.

Tom quit laughing. The other kids rustled and yawned. Mr. Cantwell had gone out for a cigarette; his coffee mug sat on the corner of his desk. Finally Tom went to the front of class and pretended to look for something near the chalkboard. Then the bell rang. He let the paper tab flutter into the mug and went back to his seat before Cantwell returned, trailing an odor of ashes.

Tom told me about it that day after school. By then the story was all over campus. Mr. Cantwell had drained his coffee without noticing the paper tab. He acted clearheaded and normal through the end of class. Then, during recess, he lost control of a cream cheese-smeared bagel. A few people who watched him try to pick it up off the pavement said Mr. Cantwell looked like a blind man, staggering around outside the teachers' lounge. He rubbed his face with a distant, agonized expression, and walked straight across campus to the football field, trotted down the bleacher steps to the track, and started running laps, with brown coattails flapping. This remedy failed, so he walked indignantly across campus again and into Mr. Cooper's (the principal's) office—out of breath by now—where he interrupted a meeting and blurted in his quacking voice, "*Mr. Cooper, I'm stoned and I'm angry!*"

A few students heard him and were given detention for laughing.

Mr. Cooper scheduled a drug-education assembly and sent a memo home to our parents. For days it was a wondered-at scandal around the neighborhood. I never told Tom this, but I was thrilled by all the uproar. It filled me with a profane joy to think the power of teachers could be overthrown so easily, and I knew Tom felt proud of his prank, and gloated, because it was such a viciously drooglike thing to do.

vii

The next day, Rachel came up to us at lunch. She stood three yards from Tom and chewed her thumbnail, holding a stack of flyers.

"Chuan says you put that tab in Mr. Cantwell's coffee," she said.

"He said that?" A smile curled on Tom's lips. "So what if I did?"

Rachel's bright black eyes studied everyone on the grass. She wore pukka shells, a hooded surf sweatshirt, and leather sandals polished at the thong by her bare skin. She gave a curt laugh. "I think you should use arsenic next time," she said quietly. Then she smiled, wide and gypsylike. "But really I just wanted to tell you about this party we're having at the end of the month. It's a Halloween party, down at Maui's place."

"Where?"

"Maui's? He lives by the beach. The address and everything is right on there."

Tom nodded impassively. "Okay."

"It's a dress-up, so you have to wear a costume."

"Okay."

He stared at the flyer. I wasn't sure if he recognized Maui's name. Most of us knew him as a Rastafarian who supplied Calaveras Beach with some of the finest Hawaiian-grown weed. He had short dreadlocks and a strong-muscled body and always wore the same pair of bright green surf trunks. On sunny afternoons he came up from the beach to a store on Pacific Avenue, speaking a happy, respectful pidgin, which his crowd of friends would translate for deli girls and clerks. He knew English, but preferred to speak his island patois. (*Jamaican* patois, it turned out.) The group would swarm in with a burst of chattering energy, clinking packs of bottles and waking up the deli, with Maui—this half-naked pauper speaking his strange and friendly pidgin—the center and source of its life.

He surfed, and made money off pot. He didn't drive. He paid little or no rent. He lived in a tiny one-room red house with a peaked roof and a front door plastered in surf stickers. Now and then he got arrested, but only on charges of minor possession, and afterwards he went back to his old business because of a firm belief that pot should be legalized. In high school these rumors had enormous cachet. I figured just showing up at his party would set me apart from the well-scrubbed masses on campus. The girls who glossed their lips and flaunted Hello Kitty notebooks, the boys who wore Bermuda shorts and looked ready for a game of golf, the New-Wave types with long, fashionable bangs—none of these people could appreciate a party at Maui's, where unruly people spilled onto the sidewalk and surfers were said to get laid.

Tom said nothing else. Rachel smiled at us. "Bring your friends," she said, and left.

I was floored, but Doug Pease didn't seem to care. "*That* sounds fun," he said. "You gonna go?"

"Maybe."

"It'll just be beer and drugs," he said in a voice that sounded, even to me, like a scolding mother. Tom stuffed the flyer in his backpack and got up to leave. For the first time I felt a clear and open allegiance with him against one of my friends.

"He's kind of a jerk, huh?" Doug said when Tom was out of range.

"He's just been through a lot. With his dad and everything."

"You don't have to apologize for him."

"I'm just saying." We were quiet for a while. Then: "Aren't you even curious about the party?"

"Like I said. It'll all be beer and drugs."

"And girls."

"And girls," he said. "Big deal."

"Like you don't care."

"Maybe I don't."

"Maybe *not*," I said suggestively.

Doug Swillinger tapped his knee. Before this argument could get any worse, the bell rang, and we all herded back to class.

viii

Nicola, I wrote that day in trigonometry. *What are you doing for Halloween?*

Nicola sat in front of me. Our classroom was an airy old space with angled-open windows. Our teacher, Mr. Dowd, was a white-haired gentleman who wielded a pointer stick and droned his explanations from the board.

I might go out to a club, she wrote back. *How come?*

I know of a costume party.

Nicola was a Goth. She had strong cheekbones, with dark and liquorish eyes that made you forget she wasn't tall. Blue-pale skin. Black hair kept short and fine as silk.

Really? she wrote. *Where?*

Down by the strand. A guy named Maui's.

Oh, that, she wrote. *I've heard about it. I might go.*

Nicola heard about most of the parties in town. She was nothing if not a socialite. Her divorced Catholic mother threw boozy soirees in the exclusive "tree section" of Calaveras Beach, and at fifteen

Nicola had a nightlife of her own, involving a cape, pale makeup, and dancing in downtown clubs. I figured she would find a costume party hard to resist.

I'm definitely going. Maybe we could have some pizza first or something.

I was sick with love for Nicola.

Or maybe Greek food?

MAYBE, she wrote. *I'll think about it.*

In history class, we'd just learned that Goths were in fact tribal Germans who lived in huts and roasted boar meat over bivouac fires. A real Goth was no more likely to wear pale makeup to a dance club and undulate in black clothes than a Viking. "Another word for 'Goth,'" I told Nicola once, "is 'Hun,'" and for a month afterward she came to school without a trace of eyeliner, wearing pressed black pantsuits worthy of a Georgetown student. She wanted to be known as foolish or trendy about as much as she wanted to be seen as ordinary or bland.

I'll dress up Goth!, I wrote.

Nicola laughed, then tapped her pen on the desk, struggling through a silent debate.

WELL, IN THAT CASE, she wrote at last. *You win. What time is this stupid party?*

ix

On Saturday Tom and I wandered onto campus and climbed a chain-link fence for a closer look at a pair of student cars. They were squarish Chrysler workhorses, painted grass-green, a school color. Faded black stencil on each door read:

CALAVERAS HIGH SCHOOL
DRIVER TRAINING
STUDENT DRIVER

Tom chuckled. A gas pump stood next to the locked school garage. The wide-swinging gate was secured with a chain.

"Doesn't Mr. Cantwell teach driver training?" he asked.

"Of course."

He went over and tested the heavy chain.

"Can you drive?" I asked.

"If it's automatic."

I peered through the window.

"It's automatic," I said.

But the chain was tight, and Tom gave up. The day was quiet and warm. From down in the Swamp we heard mourning doves flute. I wanted to mention Nicola, since she'd been on my mind all week; but any will to gossip about myself was matched by an equal and opposite desire to avoid sounding like an eager virginal boy. So I said, "You going to that Halloween thing?"

"Yeah. Are you?"

"Yup. I even found a date."

"Who?"

"This girl Nicola."

That felt cool and suave: not a hint of how I really felt.

Tom nodded thoughtfully. "You know what you're going to be?"

"I think a Visigoth."

"A what?"

"An ancient German barbarian."

X

The "tree section" of Calaveras Beach was a wealthy neighborhood of custom-designed (and therefore mismatched) houses where curled eucalyptus leaves collected in the gutters and crisped under tires and shoes. Nicola lived in a terra-cotta mansion with New Orleans-style latticework that was draped, on the night of Maui's party, in cobwebs and rubber bats. My mom steered our car into the driveway and honked. We saw movement through the blinds on the ground floor. Nicola appeared on her porch in a velvet cape and shiny silk vest.

"Ach," said my mother. "She's a vampire."

She stepped splendidly off the porch to the car. I sat in back because I needed space for my costume. "Hi, Mrs. Sperling," Nicola said as she folded herself into the passenger side—laughing, when she saw me, with what I thought was unnecessary snobbery. "What's this in your backseat?"

"I don't know, Nicola."

"I'm a Visigoth," I said.

She smiled politely and gathered her cape. Mom started driving toward the beach. "How are you, Nicola?"

"Fine."

"That's a beautiful cape."

"Thank you."

"How's school?"

"Not bad. I think I'm flunking trig, though."

"Really?" said my mom, who was easily shocked.

"Well, not flunking. I might be getting a B."

Nicola the perfectionist. She turned to look at me again. *"What* are you supposed to be?"

"A Visigoth."

We drove down to the pier, to the shop-crammed center of Calaveras Beach. Pastel-colored signs advertised bathing suits, frozen yogurt, sushi, and beer. The sun was reddening over the water. My mom stopped in front of a restaurant called The Parthenon, which gave off smells of seasoned meat. (Nicola had insisted on Greek food.)

"Home before twelve, no matter what," she said.

"I know."

"Have a good time."

"Thanks, Mrs. Sperling."

" 'Bye."

We watched her drive off. Trees along the sidewalk swayed in a briny breeze from the ocean.

"So, Eric," Nicola said tactfully, "*tell* me about this costume."

"It's my Goth costume," I said, but by now even I was losing faith. The outfit involved a phony axe, a silver spray-painted cardboard shield, fake armor, and a plastic knight's helmet from a garage sale. The main piece of clothing was a long furry singlet cut from an old coat of my mom's that looked more like carpeting than like actual animal fur. Underneath I wore beige shorts and sandals. None of it hung together well; every item seemed to have its own party to go to, and I was apparently a disgrace to be seen with. We went into The Parthenon and were seated near the window by a host with a sense of humor. Nicola fell silent, lit a clove cigarette, and stared. People on the sidewalk outside glanced up twice when they passed.

"This is embarrassing," she said.

"Sorry."

While we talked over dinner, Nicola's voice was muted, distant, and it seemed clear that my costume had scuttled my chances of kissing her later on. But the meal went smoothly enough. Before we finished, a tall homeless man pressed his face against our window. He had bright blue eyes squinting from under a fisherman's hat.

"It's Rodney," I said.

"You know him?"

"Sure, he's a local. He hangs around the pier a lot."

Through the window he said, "Halloween?" and I waved. He took his face from the window and wandered off to twist the knob of a parking meter.

"Tom and I wanted to live like Rodney when we were like eight. We tried to run away from home."

"Really?"

"Yeah, we used to go fishing with Tom's dad early in the morning, and we'd see these guys who slept under the pier walking around in tattered blankets. We thought it was a cool way to live. No parents, no responsibilities. So one day, when we were both pissed at our parents, we wrapped a bunch of things in a pillowcase and headed for the beach."

"That's cute. What kind of things?"

"Like a pocketknife. My catcher's mitt. Swim trunks. Peanut-butter sandwiches."

"That's so cute."

I shrugged. "It didn't seem cute at the time. We were pretty serious about it."

"Even cuter."

I'd forgotten how desperately eight-year-old Tom had wanted to run away. He'd been serious about hating his parents. It wasn't cute at all.

Soon we paid the bill and left. The fading sun had sunk the town under a greyish dusky half-light, and salt air from the ocean was stinging cold. We were already on Pacific Avenue, about three blocks from the party; we could smell pot and hear reggae throbbing from Maui's open windows. An orange sodium-vapor light on the curb cast a dull glow on the sidewalk and on the handful of people milling by the door. One girl at the doorway wore a tight-fitting black bodysuit and greasepaint to make her face resemble a skull. I realized only after she smiled that it was Rachel. "Hi," she said to me, drink in hand. "Did you just get here? I forget your name."

"Eric. And this is Nicola."

"Hi, nice costume," she said to Nicola.

"Thanks, you, too."

And to me: "Did you come with Tom?"

"No. I think his mom's driving him."

We went in. Maui's living room teemed with costumes and smelled like sweat and fabric and makeup and pot. The house was really a cottage; except for a bathroom at the back, next to a linoleum-tiled kitchen, it consisted of a large square living room furnished with a TV, an old coffee table, and a ruined couch. Maui sat on the couch in a jester's cap, wearing a shirt and pants but no shoes. He held a beer and chatted with three women dressed like prizefighters.

"Here's the beverages," Rachel said, guiding us to the kitchen. We each took a bottle from a stock in the fridge. "If you want to get high, just talk to Maui. He's in charge of all that stuff."

Nicola tilted up her bottle and seemed to pour the beer straight down her throat, but I took tiny sips that gave me heartburn. Almost immediately I felt like an enormous dork at that party, a clumsy Visigoth who couldn't even handle his beer. But the first thing I saw when we turned to face people again was Tom, dressed in white, standing in the doorway with a walking stick and bowler hat. He was the elegant spitting image of a droog. I went up to him and saw combat boots on his feet and long false lashes on one eye, a tiny detail that seemed almost over-shrewd, diabolical, because for Tom to put so much effort into such a small thing meant he was probably obsessed. He scanned the party, squint-eyed; his defensive guard was up but something about him looked at home in the noise and chaos of the room, the pungent odor of pot, and the reggae. I was impressed. At the sight of me, he bent over laughing.

"What the *fuck!*" he hollered, brushing his fingers on my singlet. "You're fuzzy! You're like Hagar the Horrible!"

To my horror, Nicola laughed with delight.

"How'd you get here?" I tried to change the subject.

Tom lifted his eyebrows and smiled. After another look around the room he said, "Come look," and turned to leave. I glanced at Nicola; she shrugged, so I followed him out the door.

xi

Late that afternoon Tom had watched Mr. Cantwell's driver training class pull into the open parking corral, climb out of the car, and disperse. Mr. Cantwell had left the keys on a hook inside the garage. The keys weren't hidden or secured because a mechanic was normally there. Tom listened to the sound of Cantwell's dress shoes recede on the pavement, then waited for ten minutes, nervously, until he realized there was no sign of the mechanic.

Now the car squatted like a trophy in the misted orange gloom of a streetlight, maybe four blocks from Maui's.

"Holy *shit!*" I said.

"What do you think?"

"I think you're insane."

"Nobody even knows it's gone. The mechanic must have gone home early."

He looked proud. The sight of a school car outside Maui's house filled me with excitement as well as panic. But I said, "Tom, read what it says on the door. 'Calaveras High School Driver Training.' The first cop that drives by is gonna notice."

"Not in the dark."

"You're lucky you didn't get pulled over on your way here. You could get *arrested.*"

"Don't be such a weenie."

"The cops'll probably show up here tonight."

"No, they won't. How come?"

"On a noise complaint?"

Now the eyes under his bowler hat narrowed. "You think so?" He hadn't thought about a noise complaint. "Shit! Get in. We better hide it."

He slipped behind the wheel, and the massive engine roared to life. I hesitated. Pacific Avenue flowed with headlights. I was painfully aware that any pair of them could have belonged to a police cruiser. But in a blitz of bad reasoning, I convinced myself that *Tom* had stolen the car, so *I* would get off with just a warning, or some kind of fine, which my dad would have to pay. So one minute I was just a baffled Visigoth, standing in a furry singlet next to the grass–green property of the Calaveras Beach Unified High School District; the next I was an accomplice to a major crime. Tom screeched the tires and turned off Pacific Avenue toward the beach. We drove about forty miles an hour down a narrow, darkened alleyway between the carports and garage doors of houses facing the strand. On my side I noticed a teacher's brake—a broad, shoe-worn pedal of grooved steel—and crossed my ankles in a corner of the footwell to keep from touching it.

"It's all carports on this street," I said. "Go up past the pier."

The alley next to the beach intersected Calaveras Boulevard, where bars spilled people onto the sidewalk. In the green car, with my Visigoth outfit, I felt extremely visible. Tom obeyed the speed limit until we ducked into another side street.

"Here, this one." I pointed to a narrow uphill alley. "Maybe there's some parking behind those stores."

Tom swung the Chrysler up the slope. In a sudden flare, our head-lights showed the grille of a police cruiser, parked against a wall on the right. I saw the black-and-white paint job, the darkened bar of colored lights, and stood on the teacher's brake. The Chrysler bounced on its shocks.

"*Fuck*!" Tom said.

"Fuck," I said.

"Get off the brake!"

My arms felt weak and cold. I had to force my knee to unclench. Tom jerked the Chrysler into reverse and narrowly missed a car on the side street. There was a loud honk and we expected the cop to twirl his colored lights and slam on the siren. I pictured clanking handcuffs, my parents posting bail. Tom squealed the tires on his way down the side street and all I heard in the tense silence of the Chrysler was the sound of my own blood beating.

"Is he back there?"

"I don't see him."

We drove six blocks north before Tom slowed down. No one was behind us.

"Maybe the car was empty," I said.

Tom said cryptically, "Fucking *doughnut* patrol."

We parked on a narrow residential block near the water. Tom locked the car and I started back to Maui's, hoping never to see the Chrysler again. But he paused, tapping his swagger stick against his boot. In a line of clean imported cars along the curb, our green-painted hulk stood out like an ugly smear.

"We should cover it with something," he said.

"Like what?"

"Like a *car* cover."

"Tom, just leave it there. If they find it, they'll tow it back to the school. No big deal."

"But it's got our fingerprints all over it."

His eyes were serious under his bowler hat. He thudded his stick on the pavement.

"They won't find us that way, Tom. What are they gonna do, fingerprint everyone on campus?"

"What if they do?"

He looked straight into my eyes, still serious.

"Come on," I said.

"There's a cover right here."

Under a looming strand house down the street, in a carport smelling of oil, he found a car wrapped in a greenish canvas cover. When he tugged, experimentally, a sideview mirror flipped forward against the car and set off an alarm. The horn wheezed and echoed from the silent port like a mechanical goose. I helped carry the flapping green bag to the Chrysler, and it fit well enough, but the Cadillac's horn still wheezed from up the street. "This way," said Tom, and we slipped down a narrow lane to the strand. A Spanish balustrade overlooking the beach there connected to the bike path by a flight of concrete steps. We trotted down those steps to the path and headed briskly for Maui's, about nine or ten blocks to the south. Faintly, in the distance, we still heard the Cadillac's wheezing horn.

"I can't believe you stole that car," I said suddenly. "You could get me in *trouble*. We could both go to jail."

"We're not going to jail."

"But Mr. Cooper might suspend us! I can't let that happen. You probably don't care, I know. But I want to go to college someday. I'm not gonna let some stupid prank screw that up."

" 'I wanna go to college someday,' " he repeated in a nasty whine. I couldn't believe what I was hearing. The more he resisted my vision of a wasted future, the worse everything seemed.

"If I get arrested, my dad might have to post bail. Or pay a fine. If he has to do that he'll get pissed at *both* of us. You don't know what it's like owing money to my dad," I warned him. "He can make things really unpleasant."

" 'He can make things really unpleasant,' " Tom repeated.

"Besides the fact that he's not even the first guy you'll have to deal with. From now on, you'll have to worry about a cop knocking on your door in the middle of the night!"

"Eric! Give it a *rest*. Damn."

He swaggered forward, swinging his stick. I had to jog a few steps to catch up. He kept his eyes on the pavement and put all his nervous energy into long, insistent strides. Close to the pier I saw a man leaning on a handrail who looked like a spectral shabby tree, with bare arms drooping like branches from the shoulders of a vest. It was Rodney, clutching a bottle of liquor. I said hello but he just muttered furious, obscene phrases and stared at the ground. He seemed to argue in a pinched rage with imaginary people, dream-shapes or fragments of memory. I adjusted my plastic helmet, nervously, and kept walking.

South of the pier we passed a brick bathroom that reminded me of a fishing trip one foggy morning with Mr. Linden, close to this part of the beach. "Remember your dad?" I said, but Tom was in no mood to reminisce.

"Huh," he said.

The story involved Mr. Linden and a seagull. Telling it used to make Tom weak with laughter. Mr. Linden had wandered into the brick bathroom one foggy morning when the three of us were surf fishing. He found himself alone with a seagull padding around on the floor. "It had this funny look on its face, you know; it kind of tilted its head so it could stare at me with one eye. Then it flew up to the window they have up there, right above the urinals, and flapped over my head and scared me so bad I had to back away"— he told us afterwards with a startled, marveling, Dean Martin expression—"and I pissed all over the *wall*." At this point, retelling the story, Tom would start to laugh. "Then it flew around inside the bathroom, flapping and making all kinds of noise, and so I ran out, but I guess my wallet fell on the beach while I was hiking up my trousers because when I was halfway back here, I noticed it was gone."

By now Tom was normally in tears.

"Did you find it?" I asked at the time.

"Oh, you bet," said his dad, pulling the wallet from his windbreaker. "It's just a little sandy."

It occurred to me that Mr. Linden had been drunk that morning, and his mottled red face and beady eyes came back to me in such vivid relief it was almost frightening. I glanced over at Tom, but he walked with his eyes on the pavement, tensely swinging his stick. The fine-cut features under the sodium lights looked not at all like Mr. Linden's—too cold and smooth to be his—and I wondered about the gap in emotion you must feel when a person dies who acted like your father just because of a confluence of files at an adoption agency.

"That whole thing with the seagull was pretty funny," I said.

Tom just grunted.

xii

Reggae surged from Maui's windows on Pacific Avenue. The sidewalk teemed with people. Near the doorstep Nicola talked intimately with another vampire, a wispy-looking blond kid I'd never seen before.

"Where'd you go?" Nicola said, creasing her forehead.

"Sorry, we had to park Tom's car."

She seemed mad at me, but out of fear or self-defense I decided the feeling was mutual. True, I'd left the party without telling her; but who was this vampire kid? I felt betrayed, even a little heartbroken.

Rachel came out holding a highball glass. She looked, if possible, sexier than before. Breasts and hips swayed under the tight black suit, and her slender fingers, decorated with turquoise Mexican rings, wrapped gracefully around the glass. Rachel always wore a frank expression that dared you to look anywhere besides her face. Tom drank in her whole body, and Rachel invited us in for drinks.

Twice as many people crowded Maui's little house. It was hot, and there was a plasma of want in the room, a mixture of thick leafy smoke and the odor of beer, of girls' bodies dancing and a line for cocaine at the bathroom door. It quickened my blood and made me restless to get out of my Visigoth suit. Squeezing through the costumes I could only catch a few scraps of something Rachel was saying. "He lived on Maui for a while. It's a nickname . . . It's like advertisement for his pot—'Maui brings you Hawaiian-grown,' or whatever." Tom nodded and watched Maui dance in the middle of the room. The jester's bells bounced against his waxy deep skin and he was exhaling a white gout of pot smoke, adding to the overhead fog.

"What's his real name?" I asked when I reached the fridge, but no one could hear me over the stereo. Rachel was talking to Tom in a near-whisper, her eyes round and conspiratorial. I took a beer and stood by myself for a while. Nicola had stayed outside.

For ten minutes I wrestled with a strong desire to punch her vampire friend in the nose, and maybe I should have done it—if only because a self-motivated social disaster would have improved on the bizarre and finally disastrous things that would happen later on. I know it's useless to speculate about parallel histories, or how your life might have been different; but this lull in the party strikes me as a classic example of Eric Sperling's shlemielhood, his capacity for waiting in the middle of a busy road for fate to plow him over. Because just as I was failing to make up my mind about Nicola's treachery, an aloof figure drifted toward us from the door, wearing tiny mirrored sunglasses, motorcycle boots, and a piano-key scarf. His name was Rick Fisher. He must have been twenty-five or twenty-six, like Maui, with a serious alternative profile in Calaveras Beach. Certain kids thought of him as a hugely successful artist who designed concert posters for punk and ska bands. His hair was oiled; his face looked craggy and pale. When someone introduced him to Rachel and Tom he gave a crooked, superior smile.

"Nice costume," he said. "Stanley Kubrick's a friend of mine."

"Oh, yeah?"

"He comes into my tattoo shop whenever he's in L.A."

"You have a tattoo shop?" said Rachel.

"Sure, I run a parlor in West Hollywood. Stanley's into tattoos."

I moved closer to the conversation, impressed by the way Rick had managed to make his sleazy threads look like a witticism simply by putting them on his back. He had a presence that reminded me of Nicola's, an urban intensity drawn from the contrast between pale skin and powerful eyes—Rick's were a narrow intelligent iguana green—which made them both look taller, somehow, than they really were.

After a few minutes, I heard him invite Rachel and Tom to a club in West Hollywood. "I know of a band that's playing pretty near my place. If you get bored here, let me know."

"What band?"

"They're called Felonious Punk. Down at The Garage. I'll pay the cover." He shrugged. "If you get bored."

xiii

We spent another hour at Maui's, but nothing much happened, and the house got so crowded that Rick's offer seemed hard to resist. We decided to go with him. His car was a chunky old Impala with bucket-shaped taillights and a coat-hanger antenna. I sat in back with Rachel, who had washed the greasepaint off her face. She still wore the bodysuit. Most of my costume had been dumped in a garbage can outside Maui's house.

Visiting The Garage with Rick amounted to our debut in underground society. People in the black-walled room wore trench coats, leather jackets, tinted hair, checkered pants, lensless fashion glasses, flannel shirts, nose rings, and hair sculpted like peacocks' tails. Rick hung out on the ragged edge of fashion, where any classifiable look self-destructed as soon as it threatened to become a trend. It was daunting but exciting. It made me think of that passage by Emerson about "simple purpose" and "iron necessity." This club looked to me like a sampling of a whole underworld of people who were doctrine, society, law, to themselves.

Onstage the band was setting up, forty minutes late. The drummer thumped his bass drum, the bass player thrummed, a high-booted woman with black hair said, "Check. Check," into the mike. At last Rick sat down. The band started. Noise blew from the speakers like an ill wind. The singer screeched and rolled her eyes, forming words I couldn't make out. Rick nodded his head. For twenty minutes the room shook, and no one could talk without shouting. I pretended to like it, but the music was really no good until a blond woman got up from behind the bar. "This is Jessica. She wants to do a few songs," the booted woman said, and Jessica took the microphone, traded jokes with the band, and in one stroke transformed their loose noise into a pounding, quavering bedrock for her hoarse, ecstatic voice. The room was electrified. Jessica had a sweet, lightly freckled face—not pretty but frank, with level blue eyes that lit up girlishly whenever she finished and found the audience applauding. She would shade her face with one hand to look at us under the spotlight, smile, and then launch into another song. I sensed that all the sourness and chaos from Felonious Punk, all the posing and bad attitude in the club, put up with itself just for moments like these, alive with catharsis and rapture.

When the band stopped, Jessica headed for the door. Rick

watched her go. She was tall; her powerful hips worked under a pair of leather pants.

"You feel like going outside?" Rick said. "I need some air."

The Garage opened onto an alley. Damp brick walls reflected a dim shine from streetlights on Sunset Boulevard; a Dumpster gave off the stink of rotting vegetables. Rick leaned against a drainpipe and offered me a cigarette, looking sag-eyed and drunk. We shared his whiskey, and while the hip flask passed back and forth we heard retching behind the Dumpster. Jessica came out, hair tied in a messy knot, eyes glimmering.

"Oh—sorry about that, guys. Didn't know I had company. I had to get rid of some bad liquor."

"Hey, Jessica, it's Rick Fisher."

She squinted, then: "Oh my *God!*" and they embraced. Until that moment, Rick had seemed to me like a disinterested uncle, almost asexually cold. Now I realized that inviting me outside had been a smooth scheme, a pretext for talking to Jessica.

"Are you gonna sing again?"

"Probably not. I just came to see Felonious. I was kind of drunk when I went on. I didn't even know I was gonna sing with the band tonight."

"They're your band, too, right?"

"Yeah, they play behind me. Except the bassist."

While they talked, I wondered if I was having an Authentic Downtown Experience. A familiar blend of fear and excitement stirred in me. I pressed the light on my watch. Almost eleven. I worried about getting home. Rick led us back into The Garage, and after a few minutes, he invited everyone back to his apartment "to decompress." This was another scheme—an obvious pass at Jessica. I wanted to leave, but Rachel and Tom were enthusiastic, so we piled into Rick's Impala for the short ride to his apartment. He parked in front of a pale stucco shoebox of a building with two black iron starburst lights clinging to the wall like abalone shells.

Rick's place, on the second floor, was dim-lit and cluttered with sketchpads and laundry. I sat next to Rachel on a short leather couch by the window, where curtains caught the whitish glare from outside. Tom sat next to her; the three of us were crammed on the couch. A bong stood in the middle of an ash-streaked coffee table, and its presence in the middle of the room might have been amiable, like a hookah, except for the murky, sewerish water at the bottom. It was a blue Plexiglas tower with extra bowls and bits of resin littered around the base.

Rick put a record on the stereo and said, "If you feel like smoking, we can fire up the bong."

Soon smoke was coiling around the apartment with a dry tumbleweed smell. In that warm haze my hand couldn't keep from touching Rachel's Lycra-wrapped leg. Tom was right next to her, but she seemed to respond, even flirt back. My heart skipped.

We heard voices outside the door. There was a knock and a yell—"Ricky!"—and Rick opened up to let three of his friends file in. One had a partially shaved head with little pigtails tied off at random by colorful rubber bands. His eyes were small and blue and he wore combat fatigues. Another was effeminate and thin, wearing sunglasses. The third looked like Rick, only his name was Dale.

"Have a seat," said Rick, and Kevin, the man in pigtails, flopped into one armchair. Dale squeezed next to me, and the effeminate man, Miles, watched us with a blank, mincing reserve, not deigning to take off his glasses. All three of them gave off a miasma of attitude and danger that withered any hope I still had of getting home on time. Jessica watched the strangers with her forward, glimmering eyes. Then she asked about the bathroom. Rick told her where it was.

"So what's new, Ricky?" Kevin said when she was gone. "What'd you do tonight?"

"Went to The Garage. Saw Felonious Punk."

"Any good?"

"Not bad. Jessica showed up unannounced. She put on a fantastic show."

They talked a little more. I pressed the light on my watch—quarter to twelve. I was about to ask Rick about that ride home when he excused himself to "see about Jessica," and we were left alone with his friends.

Rachel repacked the bong. Miles took off his blazer; I saw a black lining shimmer expensively under the dim light. The black fabric of Rachel's bodysuit also shimmered, and my arm was crushed against her. Tom sat two feet away. I felt aroused, curious, and scared. His attention was on the conversation, not what Rachel and I were doing. But I noticed that if I let my hand linger on Rachel's thigh—if I made it anything more than an unconscious touch—she recoiled, as if touching was okay, but *knowing* about it was unacceptable. My blood pounded.

Kevin pulled out a personal calendar and started to draw. The sight of a man with a shaved head and pigtails writing in an Organizer made his friends chuckle.

"I love to doodle when I'm stoned," he said.

"Oh, *please*," Miles sneered. "You've been carrying that thing around for *ages*."

"Only for two months. And I stole it from you."

"You did not. I never owned such a thing."

"Yes, you did. You brought it home from the office one day and left it on the counter. It sat there for *ages*." Kevin was mocking. "And you never even noticed it was gone."

"It must have been a present from a Christmas party. We have one of those grab-bag things at the office where I work." Miles sighed. "It's so stupid. The year before last, I got a desk set, you know, with pens and a little letter opener? I don't know *who* thinks these things are good gifts. They must make the rounds, from one Christmas party to another."

"You did that yourself. You brought it to another party, like the week after."

"Well, yes I did, Kevin, and my girlfriend's manager was fucking happy to get it."

Miles adjusted his sunglasses and gazed at Dale. We were following the conversation, stoned and accepting, but now Miles looked as if a staggering idea had made him fall silent. Dale stared back. He wore black jeans and a short T-shirt showing his upper-arm tattoos, like Rick. He had leather motorcycle boots and his hair was dark. But it wasn't slick—that was one difference—and his brown eyes had a round, almost teddy-bear earnestness.

Miles said, "Should we break out the powder?"

Dale shrugged. "It's your stuff."

"Where's Rick, anyway? I thought we'd share."

"I think I heard him go into his bedroom."

"Really? With Jessica?"

"Whoever."

"Ricky?" Miles called, straining his delicate voice.

No answer.

"He's involved," said Kevin. "Break out the stuff."

Miles drew an elegant silver-plated tray with flared edges from his blazer, then rooted in a pocket for a Ziploc bag of white dust. He laid everything on the coffee table and glanced at us. "You like cocaine?"

"Sure," Tom said.

I gave him a look, but his expression was cool. Bluffing.

"Well, if you're interested, this is primo shit." He poured a pile onto the silver-plated tray. "Prime Colombian cola," he bragged.

"Miles can afford it because his parents are rich," said Kevin.

"Miles can afford it because Miles has a *job*," said Miles.

From a cigarette case in his blazer, he drew a razor blade, and cut the pile of powder into twelve even lines. His fingers were deft, caressing, and to our pot-hazed minds they were a floor show to focus on while we thought about sniffing cocaine. The warm crush of Rachel's body and my free-floating terror of Tom made my heart race. The whole evening had stretched my nerves past their usual limits. Never mind the stolen Chrysler, or Nicola's treachery; never mind my stupid costume or the pressure of flirting with Rachel; the combination of these things plus our failure to get home on time—and now the drugs from these friends of Rick's—put so much stress on my German-Jewish sense of order that my brain felt ready to pop.

"Where do you work?" Tom asked quietly.

"Me?" Miles glanced up. "Fucking Paramount Records. I've been there for three years, and I hate it."

"It's a good job," Kevin said. "I'd hang onto it."

"We'll see."

"It's money," said Kevin.

"There's that." Miles shrugged, concentrating on the lines of powder. "I want to run my own label."

Rachel was still aware enough of my body to squirm away whenever we got too comfortable, but her reactions had slowed. Her body felt warm and relaxed. The tension in the room was as muted and low-burning as the overhead light, and Rachel's red-rimmed eyes, staring at the coke, showed wariness verging on fear. Tom's showed hunger. Dale circulated the bong again I declined and passed it to Rachel, then started nervously stroking her thigh.

"This stuff comes from a guy I know in Burbank," Miles went on. "He's Nicaraguan or something. Fat guy with a mustache. He gets the purest coke in southern California."

"What's his name?" said Dale.

"Cándido Flambón."

"I thought you got your stuff from that guy under the freeway."

Miles looked up. "Well, that's how big this guy is. He's Freeway

Rick's supplier." He turned to us. "Have you ever heard of Freeway Ricky Ross?"

We shook our heads.

"He's the main coke salesman for all of downtown L.A. Most of his customers are in South Central. They're all into rock now, rock cocaine? Freeway says he doesn't have time to deal with me anymore, so he put me in touch with his boss. Anyone bigger than Freeway has *got* to be huge, and this guy gets the coke straight from Central America. It's as pure as can be."

Miles tapped the razor on the plate and sat up in his armchair.

"Okay," he said. "Ready?"

What happened next is hard to remember in detail. Kevin refused the bong, so Tom stood up to set it on the coffee table, but just as he did, Rachel seemed to notice—with the delayed reaction of a stoned person—that I was publicly, brazenly petting her leg. She jerked sideways and jostled Tom, who lost control of the bong and toppled it toward Miles's silver tray. No one moved fast enough to catch it. The tube not only caught one flared edge of the tray and launched all twelve lines of coke into the air—spilling water onto the floor next to Miles—it also crushed the open Ziploc bag and discharged a cloud of white powder into his lap, dusting his tailored slacks and settling on the puddle of bong water to form a bitter greyish mud. I remember uproar, hysteria. The night was crowned at last with the disaster I'd been expecting all along. I remember Kevin howling an outraged hyena laugh; I remember Tom trying to apologize while Rick came out of his bedroom and Jessica stood in his doorway, half-dressed, with an odd, incongruous smile. I remember Miles packing up what was left in his plastic bag and storming out with his mouth full of inconsolable rage, kicking at the doorway and asking Tom if he knew what kind of a fuckhead he was and how much money he'd just scattered all over the fucking furniture? And I remember going home in Rick's car, baffled and silent, weirdly satisfied, in a daze.

I was grounded for two weeks. Tom and I were both grounded, in fact, in my bedroom, two Saturdays in a row, while our mothers had lunch on the deck. On the second Saturday, I sat at my desk doing homework while Tom stretched across the covers of my bed in jeans and checkered Vans, staring at a squadron of model planes that hung from my ceiling. Soon he rolled my basketball around from under the bedstand and bounced it hard on the carpet. Then he announced that he going to ask Rick for a job.

"At his tattoo studio? How come?" I said.

"I need money. I want to start doing stuff with Rachel. I'll need money for that."

"What stuff?"

"Going out and stuff. Women cost money, Eric."

"Like you know anything about it."

"More than *you.*"

Bounce.

"I mean, I really like her," he said. "I want to *do* stuff for her."

"Really?"

He nodded, looking serious, and raised his eyebrows.

"It's weird."

They'd been going out for a full week.

"Have you had sex yet?"

"Yeah." He smiled.

I turned back to my trig homework. The blood ran to my face, and my ears felt hot. A year younger than me, and he loses his virginity just like that? Little bastard. I was too proud to ask for details.

"Also," Tom added, "that guy Miles wants money from me."

"You're kidding. For the coke?"

"Yeah, he's still pissed. He called information for my phone number."

"How much do you owe him?"

"Almost a thousand bucks."

"Jesus, Tom!"

He nodded and bounced the basketball. "If I get a job with Rick," he said, "I figure he could give Miles the money up front, and let me work it off."

"That's clever." I paused. "Is Rick even hiring?"

"I still have to ask him."

The idea of telling Tom it was my fault crossed my mind like the shadow of a blimp, remote and silent. But I said nothing. It was too hard to explain.

"What'd you do with the car?" I asked.

"It's still parked by my place, on some little street. Under the cover."

"You gonna return it?"

He shrugged. "I don't know. It's safe where it is right now. I might keep it. I mean it's a great car—it runs fast." He folded his arms under his head and smirked. Now he seemed less like a scrappy little punk and more like a self-reliant young lion, testing his cunning and prowess by keeping a stolen car.

"That's grand theft auto," I pointed out.

"Only if I get caught."

I laughed. "You'll get caught as soon as you take off that cover."

"I can paint it."

"With what paint?"

"Paint's not too hard to find, Eric. I'll figure out something."

He was always a step ahead, no matter what we did. I was thrilled and repelled by the idea of Tom keeping that car.

"I don't think you have the guts to steal the Chrysler," I said now. "You just think you do because of Harold or whatever."

"What do you mean?"

"It's something Harold and his friends would do."

"*Tch.*"

"Or it's like *A Clockwork Orange*."

He laid his head down again, shook it in little twitches, and stared up at the plastic planes. After a few seconds, he said in a sudden nasty passion, "What makes you think you're so *smart*, Eric? You might be good in school, but you're a goddamn coward. *You're* the one who wouldn't have the guts to steal a car, not even if you wanted to. You're too much of a sheep."

"What do you mean, sheep?"

"You're a conformist. You want people to *like* you, so you do what they want."

I creased my forehead.

"And there's nothing worse than being a conformist around *here*. I mean, most people in Calaveras Beach just go along with whatever's around and try to be liked."

I watched him.

"You're just greedy," I said.

He narrowed his eyes. "And you think too much. You bury your nose in your books, but you don't know a thing about life. You can't criticize me."

Tom had a quick instinct for weakness. I wasn't sure what to say.

"You're the kind of person things just *happen* to," he went on. "You're exactly the kind of guy Nietzsche would have hated. You know who Nietzsche was, smart guy? He was a *philosopher*. And he thought people who were too weak to assert themselves were *fuckheads*."

Tom was possessed with a sudden, temperamental rage. My small show of defiance must have set him off. I'd never heard philosophy from him before, though sometimes he quoted Jim Morrison.

"Well, at least I'm not a car thief," I said bitterly.

"Tch," said Tom. "You're not *free*."

On the Monday after Maui's party, Nicola came in late to trigonometry, gripping the strap of her bag like a chairwoman late for a meeting. "Hi," she breathed, and turned her back. I saw nothing but her pale, graceful neck for the rest of class. She opened her textbook, paid attention, and even raised her hand twice to give an answer.

"That's right," Mr. Dowd said. "Glad to see you're with us today, Miss Greaves."

I passed her a note:

How's it going?

When she felt my tap on her shoulder she half-turned her head and took it from me delicately. But an answer never came. I wrote a second one that was more to the point.

Who was that vampire?

She took this note with the same reluctant sneak of her right hand. The white-haired Mr. Dowd, with his thick glasses and drooping jowls, droned on and tapped on the blackboard.

Finally Nicola wrote back:

Her name's Sarah.

Sarah!

I wrote, *The vampire was a girl?*

YES, she's a girl. Young woman.

Mr. Dowd stared at me and I stared back, full of this new information. The sun outside the door angled under the heavy overhang and glared off the slabs of concrete in front of our room.

So you're a lesbian? I wrote.

Her reply took a minute, but it was unequivocal.

Shut up, Eric.

I crumpled the note and backed off. After a while, feeling conciliatory, I wrote,

How do you know her?

I met her before in a club. She's weird. She's not really sure what she wants to be.

What do you mean?

You know. Lesbian, or—not.

I watched Mr. Dowd at the blackboard.

How could she not know?

Nicola scribbled for a long time, then reached the paper back to me under her armpit. Apparently, it was my week for being explained to:

It's complicated, *Eric. Even if you think you are lesbian, or gay, or whatever, then you have to deal with coming out to your parents, your friends, and all the social bullshit that goes along with that. I mean you can't even get married if you're homosexual. Did you know that? It's so stupid. It's okay to have a sex change, and once you get a sex change it's okay to get married, but if two people who happen to like sleeping with each other even though they happen to be the same gender want to get married, they can't. This country is so* fucked up!

I wrote, *A lot of countries are like that. Not just this one.*

Nicola looked back at me after she read that; her forehead glowered fiercely.

It's bigoted. *I don't care how many countries are like that, it's* wrong.

It might be wrong, I wrote.

It's worse than bigoted, it's completely fucked!

Nicola reached around for the piece of paper before I could answer and snatched it from me.

But anyway, she wrote, *once you get past all* that, *then you have to wonder why you* are *gay—or lesbian, or whatever—and that's what Sarah's dealing with. She read some psychological bullshit that said homosexuals were just narcissists, like they just want to be with someone who's made in their own image. That's pretty disturbing. I mean, what if somebody told you the only reason you wanted love is because you're* vain?

All this was beyond my experience of either sex or love, and I was still staring at the sheet of paper when the bell rang.

part three

xvi

It's late in the evening; the last of the sun has left a blood-orange band across the horizon. I can't help noticing that Rodney has fallen asleep. Sandflies swirl around his handlebar mustache, his hat has flopped beside him on the beach. He snores a little. To be absolutely honest, I don't know when he drifted off.

• • •

The Zohar is hard to read in this dusk, and most of it, anyway, is too obscure to understand. I'd like to visit Rabbi Gelanter for advice, but he moved away from Calaveras Beach a few years ago. His free-form lectures were always more interesting than any of the books he gave us to read. The lectures were not part of class; they happened when one of us visited him to get a form signed, or to ask some simple question. I remember him leaning back behind his messy desk to give long, esoteric replies. He cracked open pistachios while he talked.

One of the things he said was that the soul consisted of seeing, or perception. All three levels dealt with different kinds of perception: The *nefesh* took in sensory things, like pleasure and pain. The *ruach* weighed and judged, and the *neshamah* engaged in sophisticated reasoning. I remember Rabbi Gelanter gesturing with his powerful arms and licking bits of pistachio from his beard as he explained that the more fundamental levels of the soul were also less individual—

you moved along the hierarchy from *nefesh* to *neshamah* and found less room for "me" or "mine." What you found instead, he said, was an intense light, a burning, like an eager candle flame.

He always rambled this way, with no encouragement from me. That may have been part of the point. Did he expect a twelve-year-old to understand these arcane ramblings about the soul? No, he just needed to work it out for himself, explicate to the walls while I sat, politely, listening. I must have impressed people in general as some kind of blank slate, an innocent boychik who had to be told things, instructed, because people were always lecturing me.

Still, the lectures had an influence. What I took from him was over-simple, and not too well thought out, but my trouble with Tom came down to a basic disagreement about what it meant to be a man. For me it meant a cramped kind of self-effacement or self-sacrifice. For Tom it was about self-assertion. He wanted to swagger about the earth like a giant. Every boy wants that—and I was no exception—but I had the idea that I was better than he was in a few important respects. First of all, I was smarter: I wanted to go to college and find a good job as a professor or surgeon or something. I could afford to be patient and self-effacing. Second, I was *morally* better than Tom; for years I'd restrained myself as a well-behaved mama's boy, and those sacrifices had not been forgotten. At some point in the shimmering future I expected to bathe in the spoils due to all good princelings and martyrs.

• • •

My old house is a half-hour walk from the pier, first under the sodium lights of Calaveras Boulevard and then along Pacific Coast Highway, past the white-lit auto showrooms and neon restaurants that seem to doze under a salted, sea-smelling mist. Our stretch of Pacific Coast Highway is nothing like the legendary road through Malibu, along those dramatic mud-sliding cliffs and precarious houses. It's a dingy business strip, with low-rise office buildings, fast-food joints, and a few Jiffy Lubes.

Now it must be eight or nine o' clock. The Swamp at this hour feels eerie, dangerous. I catch myself wondering what or who could be hiding behind the pale shadows of eucalyptus. Nelson Street is busy with TVs in the windows. Junipers, olive trees, and low-hanging bottlebrush obscure the houses. There's a wrought-iron fence around my parents' lawn, and the place itself is a beige stucco bungalow with a wooden veranda on the left, and a few Spanish touches—ornamental tiles, stone urns on the porch—that must have been stylish in the 1950s, when this part of town was built.

Right now my dad's in the garage. A radio emits a murmuring stream of news. While I was alive he always kept a single radio going in the bedroom upstairs, but now, ever since the accident, radios in the kitchen, the bathroom, the study, and the garage give off a sober chorus of cultural programming my dad can listen to from any part of the house. I doubt he even pays attention. He just needs the presence of voices. Sometimes he forgets to switch off a radio before going to bed, so the voices murmur for hours on end to the car, or the curtains in the study, or the bathroom linoleum.

I stand halfway down the driveway and watch. His lamp shines from the workbench.

Dad grew up around Newark in the 1940s and 1950s, part of the same generation as Rabbi Gelanter. He was the first son of Orthodox Jews who'd fled Warsaw in World War II, and he came west to work for TRW, an aerospace company, in 1964. The company sent him to Germany to help with some big NATO project—he was part of a band of engineers who later made up my parents' circle of friends—and he met my mom in a Berlin café. My mom appears in pictures from that time as a flinty, short-haired, sweet-smiling woman, wearing cat's-eye sunglasses and white cardigan sweaters. She wasn't Jewish, and the idea of my dad marrying a

German *shiksa* appalled his parents in Jersey. There were loud, long-distance arguments on the phone, followed by a hasty marriage. I know that for them to marry out of simple love within twenty years of World War II was a hopeful thing to do; it was like Yehudi Menuhin, the Jewish violinist, playing with the Berlin Philharmonic in 1947. It took courage. But my parents also wanted the past to be done with, forgotten, which is one reason they settled in the bland paved hangover of postwar L.A.

Dad's black hair has turned peppery white. He has stooped shoulders, responsibility-ridden brown eyes, and a thick mustache like Groucho Marx. Right now—around nine on a Tuesday night—he's fixing a length of sprinkler pipe.

I watch him for a while, then turn for the wooden deck and slip into the house through a rickety French door.

"Walter?" my mother says from the living room.

To my left is the kitchen, and beyond that, on a low mezzanine, my mom has been sitting on the sofa, reading the *Los Angeles Times* under a hideous, heavy, burnished-gold lamp my grandparents sent us on Hanukkah. It was a welcome-mom-to-the-family gesture, circa 1976.

"Walter?"

She comes down the mezzanine steps and stands on the kitchen floor, arms crossed and wrapped in the sleeves of a cardigan, looking worried and cold. Her bright face has fallen into a mask of light wrinkles and brooding lines. She has short white hair. Her frame is short and birdlike.

"I thought I heard something," she says to herself, and puts on a kettle for tea.

From the living room I hear strains of *Tristan and Isolde*. Mom listens to opera the way dad listens to radio news. Her classical-music collection is vast, and *Tristan and Isolde* reminds me of the time I decided to join the marching band in junior high. (Somehow Mom never had a lot of patience for her own son's interest in music.) This won't be the most flattering story, for either of us, but here it goes: She came home from work one day and found me trying to play the tuba. She looked in at the door to my room, frowned, and asked what I was doing. When I told her, she wondered if the school wouldn't rather have a pianist.

"For a marching band?"

"That piano in the living room can be tuned," she suggested.

"I don't think Mr. Hendersen needs any pianos in the marching band."

"Have you asked him?"

"No."

When I kept up with the tuba, for the rest of that week, she countered with housework. First she vacuumed in the hall outside my door; then she asked me to take out the garbage. When I promised to do it "soon," and went on practicing, she faded into the living room to lie in curtained gloom with *Tristan and Isolde* on the stereo. She propped her nyloned ankles on one arm of the couch and shut her eyes, like a woman with a crippling headache. (Passive aggression must run in the family.) When I came into the kitchen for a glass of water, I would hear the opera turned just low enough to have been assaulted by my tuneless, blaring noise.

"Everything all right, Mom?"

Silence, except for Isolde dying. Then, in a thin and melancholic voice:

"Can you *please* take out the garbage?"

• • •

Anyway, I'm not sure why I came here. Watching my parents age at home is not a whole lot of fun. The old familiar odors of vacuumed carpet and steeping tea fill me with grief, and I'm not inclined to give speeches or explanations. That's beside the point now. The worst thing my parents could have imagined as a hopeful young couple in the 1960s, setting up house in L.A. and looking forward to a life in a booming country—the only thing that could have made the whole domestic enterprise feel like an absolute bust—has come to pass. What else is there to explain?

• • •

Drivers of tractors raking the beach clean of garbage every morning sometimes find tramps in the path of their headlights, and now, as the sky turns blue in the east, a sharply grumbling motor approaches from north of the pier. Soon two quivering lamps glare through the pilings onto Rodney's sleeping back. "Hey," a voice hollers. "Hey, man, you can't stay there." The tractor rips the morning with a dirty, muttering racket. Rodney stirs awake and clambers to his feet. But he's in no hurry to leave. He seems to hesitate just to show the driver a thing or two, and when he notices something at his feet, he stoops to pick it up. My library book! He shoves it into his backpack. The driver says, "Sorry, man, you can't sleep there." Rodney answers with a hoarse, curt "Go to hell."

He mounts the pier steps, and I follow him up Calaveras Boulevard. Under the deep blue sky, all the shops for bikinis, frozen yogurt, stationery, and women's shoes have a mute dignity in spite of their pastel signs. The sprawling oafish Safeway looks quiet and stern. Above the store, at the foot of a steep hill, a strip of eucalyptus trees and pines, oleanders and iceplant grow along the damp-smelling cinder bed and the railroad. This leafy corridor muffles the sound of trains. Rodney wanders into it, squats beside an oleander, and waits.

I want that book, but can't think how to take it from him.

• • •

This corridor used to be an important branch of the L.A. rail system until a homeowners' group harried Amtrak to re-route its trains. Now, in the daytime, passenger trains leave Calaveras Beach in peace, but tangle traffic in Inglewood. The trains that still have passing rights—two rusted-boxcar freights, like relics from the Depression—clack slowly through town before six in the morning. Sometimes I see Mexican immigrants riding between the cars, two or three men balancing on a single joggling hitch. They probably hop the trains near Tijuana and head straight for fields above Salinas.

The sky lightens; a blood-pink stain rises over the hill. Soon a bell at the intersection announces a train. The mellow sound of the trundling wheels and the broad sigh of the whistle excite me. Rodney lets the engine pass and gets up to trot beside the cars with a wolfish lope. He glances cannily up and down the line, looking old but well-practiced. His fisherman's hat is tucked in the waist of his dungarees. He grabs the ladder of a grain car and raises one foot to the lower rung, then clambers with a spider's grace over the side. I imitate him, with less agility but no fear for my life; and suddenly we're on the train, picking up speed, relaxed on a comfortable pile of barley.

The last time I visited northern California, to see Tom, I got there by Greyhound. Jumping a boxcar never occurred to me. But this is a better way to go—more encouraging to the memory. The sun streams over the eastern hill; eucalyptus trees wave overhead.

xvii

In the first week of November, our principal sent out a mimeo-graphed notice to explain the Chrysler's theft to our parents, and the local papers ran the story. No one suspected Tom. He kept his mouth shut out of pure fear; in fact, he would feel paranoid about the car as long as it was painted green. In the meantime, he culti-vated his new social standing. After Maui's party he suddenly had the attention and respect of a socially important crowd of people, and the effect on his personality was like the effect of water on a plant. His color improved; his posture straightened. He no longer went slinking around school like a hunted animal. He wore sloppier clothes and kept a cool skeptical look in his eyes. During lunch he ate with Rachel on the cinder-block wall. Without even wanting people to like him, it seemed, Tom had graduated to another social sphere, and from my spot on the grass it was annoying to watch him sit with a stony-faced look of entitlement while Rachel ran her fin-gers through his cropped hair or polished her sunglasses on his shirt.

But we were still friends, and on weekends we started playing basketball again. After a game one Saturday, we happened to stop into Mr. B's, where a strange man dressed in black leaned next to the register, keeping the fat man company on a slow day. At first we blew some money on the video game and didn't notice who the guy was. But when we paid for our drinks at the register, we recognized Bartholomew's friend as Rick Fisher, looking casual but relentlessly hip in black jeans and a T-shirt with the sleeves ripped off, one gold hoop earring and a piratelike bandanna over his slicked-back hair.

"Hey Rick. What are you doing here?"

He shrugged and gave us a lizard smile. "Just wasting time. I used to work for Dave, back when I was like you guys. I'd come and work here after school."

"You went to Calaveras?"

"Sure. I used to sit back here and listen to music all day. Dave used to let us bring in tapes. We'd listen to old blues and ska stuff. Skatal-ites, Otis Redding, the Wailers." He dropped these names, then sized us up with his green intelligent eyes. "What are you guys into?"

Tom said, "I'm pretty much into Black Flag," which was an

absolute lie. He hadn't heard more than a couple of Black Flag songs on the radio. But it must have seemed like a good answer because Black Flag was a rising local band. We saw their symbol spray-painted on the sidewalk or Xeroxed on telephone-pole flyers—four bars that looked like a waving flag, which stood either for anarchy or roach spray, depending on who you asked.

"Henry Rollins and that crew. They tried to go corporate." Rick nodded slowly. "I was friends with him for a while."

"Really?"

"Dave, you know Henry Rollins, don't you?" Rick said.

"Goddamn punk," said Mr. B.

"That's right." Rick smiled. "He used to rehearse in a church."

"Didn't you say you knew Stanley Kubrick, too?" I asked.

"Stanley? Sure. He comes into my shop whenever he's in L.A." Rick turned to Mr. B. "I met these guys at a Halloween party, and Tom, here, was dressed as one of those guys from *Clockwork Orange*." Bartholomew grunted. Rick pulled out a black wallet and gave us a card. "Here," he said. "That's me. Drop by anytime."

Tom stared at the design on the business card. I wondered if he was going to ask Rick for a job, but he seemed suddenly tongue-tied. He slipped the card into his pocket.

"If you guys aren't busy," Rick said, "you want to go for a ride? I happen to know Hi-Fi has some good music."

"Hi-Fi?"

"The record store?"

"We don't have any money," Tom said.

"Doesn't matter. Come on." He started to leave. "All set, Dave?"

"Yup."

We went out. Rick's old Impala glared white under the heavy afternoon sun. We sat on the hot vinyl; he plucked his tiny mirrored sunglasses from the dashboard and slid them onto his face. Music crashed from the speakers as he steered onto the road.

"So, have you seen that girl Rachel since the party?" he asked.

"Rachel? All the time,"

"She's his girlfriend," I said.

"Really?" Rick was genuinely surprised. "You weren't going out at the party, were you?"

"That's when it started."

Rick nodded and drove down Pacific Coast Highway towards the ocean, which looked white-hot, reflecting the sunlight in a rippled glare. After a while Tom said, "Are you good friends with Mr. B?"

"Yeah, we've stayed in touch since I worked for him. He's an okay guy when you get to know him. He helped me set up my shop."

"How big is your shop, anyway?"

"Pretty small, just a little storefront on Melrose." Rick opened the glove compartment. "How come?"

"I was wondering if you needed help there."

"What kind of help?" In the glove compartment he found a pack of Marlboros. "Cigarette?"

"No thanks."

Rick offered me one. When I shook my head, he lit up, with a match, taking both hands off the wheel as we coasted downhill.

"I guess I just wanted to know if you had a job open or something," Tom persisted.

"You want a job?"

"I need one. To pay back Miles."

"Has he been hassling you?"

"He's been calling my *house.*"

"Hmm." Rick adjusted his sunglasses. "I've never had like an assistant or anything, but I'll ask around." He tapped the steering wheel. "Maybe this guy Paul at Hi-Fi needs help." He took another drag on the cigarette and flung it into the road. "Stale," he explained. But Tom kept watching him expectantly. "I'll see what I can do," Rick said.

"Thanks."

The record store was tucked at the bottom corner of a tall concrete office building. It felt warm and pleasant inside. Dusty bins narrowed the room to a single aisle, and behind the counter, leaning over a newspaper, stood Paul, a stout youngish man in green plaid, with a flattop the color of brown shoe polish. Speakers mounted near the ceiling played a shambling song, a bright pumping organ behind a nasal voice. Rick introduced us, saying he wanted to lay the groundwork for our "musical initiation." We spent a few minutes flipping through bins of records. It didn't take him very long to collect a stack that included a few of the bands he'd mentioned—Otis Redding, Skatalites—along with early records by the Velvet Underground, David Bowie, The Clash, and an unknown group from Georgia called R.E.M. When I wondered what was playing over the stereo, he asked Paul to take it off and bought that, too. It was *Blonde on Blonde*, by Bob Dylan.

Paul bagged our music. Rick asked him, "Hey, do you have any room for an assistant?"

"What kind of an assistant?"

"This guy needs a job."

Paul glanced up at Tom, looked sympathetic, but shrugged. "Sorry, I barely have room for a cash register."

"We'll think of something," Rick promised.

He must have recognized in both of us the sort of kid he used to be, a beach-city innocent who looked up to adults like him. He showed us music that made more sense than anything we heard on the radio; he introduced us to a grown-up version of our own discontent. To us, a man like Rick Fisher, who exuded grim integrity like a modern-day Shane, seemed streetwise enough to reveal whatever our neighborhood was concealing from us about Real Life.

"Oh, shit, is that the right time?" he said suddenly, pointing at a clock on the wall.

"Afraid so. How come?" said Paul.

"I forgot I had to get to my parents' place before three." He was half an hour late. "You have to be home right away?" he asked us.

"No."

"Not *right* away."

"Can you do me a favor? In exchange for the records? Do you mind coming up to my folks' place on Soledad? I can drive you home right afterwards."

I looked at Tom. This was an offer we were supposed to refuse—a ride to the house of a strange older man—but Rick had been honest and decent so far. He'd been generous, in fact, and as commanding of respect as a cool older brother. Tom and I were a little awed.

"Sure."

"Sure."

"I'm taking care of my parents' place for a couple of weeks," he explained. "I have to let the dog out twice a day because otherwise she shits on the carpet."

We followed Rick to the car. He steered the old Impala down Pacific Coast Highway and turned up a winding, juniper-fragrant hill road. Mt. Soledad was a lush and quiet mountain peninsula built up with expensive homes.

"Where'd your parents go?" I asked.

"Costa Rica. They're on vacation for a month."

The Fishers were obviously loaded. They lived in the heart of Mt. Soledad, across from an open, still-undeveloped field of brush and manzanita. The house was sprawling, sunken, with a concrete porch set between a bright blue fish pool and a planter full of lilies and ferns. Two strips of polished amber glass flanked the door. Behind it, we heard a collar chain jangle. Rick opened the door and a beagle jumped against his legs, growling and snuffling with pleasure. "Hey, Sadie. What's happening, Sadie," he said, and

Sadie sniffed everyone's knees before running into the kitchen. A marble-floored entryway swam back into a shadowy, green-furnished living room. There was the smell of teak furniture, deep rich upholstery, and distinctly—from the direction of the living room—fresh dog shit.

"Sadie!" Rick started to call, following her into the kitchen. "You're a bad dog—*bad dog.*"

We heard whimpering.

"Sorry about this, guys." Rick came out of the kitchen with a handful of paper towels. Sadie followed him, looking penitent. In his torn black T-shirt, smirking and bouncing hesitantly on his feet, Rick wiped up the mess on his parents' living-room carpet and carried the shit-heavy bundle through a sliding glass door. He whacked Sadie on one haunch and shooed her outside, then found a sponge in the kitchen to clean the stain. "I wasn't supposed to let that happen," he said. "If you guys wanna relax for a minute, you can. There's some beers in the fridge. And you can put those records on the stereo."

We took two bottles of Michelob from Rick's fridge and put on the records. The Fishers had a trim black stereo set into a teak sideboard. Rick turned it up so we could hear it from the backyard pool. Not every adult would have paid his own money to buy us music he simply thought we should hear (and Rick had made this sound like a moral issue) before bringing us to his parents' elegant home and offering us alcohol to make up for a difficult situation. It seemed too good to be true. Here was a man who'd been raised in our suburb without developing the prejudices of our parents, and his stripped-down attitude gave him an irresistible glamour, the cruel romantic sheen of a man who could see through all the social-climbing bullshit of his hokey hometown.

Relaxed on a patio chair while Sadie trotted around the pool, Rick talked for a while about his own high-school career. "One summer vacation I went to a show in New York, at a smoky little club with, like, two hundred seats," he said in a reflective voice, "and saw two singers. One of 'em was Bob Marley. He played this island music that was closer to ska than reggae. And he opened for a scruffy beatnik named Bruce Springsteen. Back then Springsteen was still pretty cool, melodic and smart, a good songwriter. His live act had a lot of funky energy, it wasn't like that freight-train thing he does now. He sang with Lou Reed on one of his albums."

Rick took a swig of beer. The dog's collar tags jangled as she trotted around the pool. "*Sadie!*" She stopped, stared over her shoulder. "Calm down." He tapped his bottle with one long fingernail. "It was a weird time. The early seventies. It was like all the fears of the sixties were coming true. Jimi Hendrix and Janis Joplin had just died, Nixon was about to self-destruct, Vietnam was still going on. . . . As a freshman I figured I was gonna go to college and be in a fraternity, go to football games like most of my friends. But then I learned a thing or two about music, a thing or two about politics, I learned what was really going on. . . ."

The dog started running again. "Sadie!" Rick shouted. "Cut it out!" He tipped up his beer. "I don't know, college just seemed like a joke. It was ridiculous, especially after Watergate. It seemed like playacting. I decided not to participate. I started going to shows and even playing in my own band for a while. . . . I played drums. I thought I was a mod Charlie Watts." He gave a low dark laugh. "Luckily I knew how to draw, though. If it wasn't for art school I'd be a bum living down by the beach."

He was happy to have an audience, someone to hear his life story explained from just the right angle. He went on for half an hour. It never occurred to me that one reason Rick dazzled us was that the Fishers were already rich. They were through with social climbing, so Rick's main business was to fall picturesquely away from his privileges. None of this would be clear for a long time. While we sat by the pool with our beers, in fact, listening to a strange man in a cutoff T-shirt, motorcycle boots, and a pirate earring explain to us about his misspent youth, it was actually kind of a riddle.

Still, the insurrectionary jangle of those albums Rick bought us fired my blood. To me the best line came in Dylan's "Absolutely Sweet Marie." The voice was chiding, ironic, angry, but liberated, and one line rang out like a gunshot:

But to live outside the law, you must be honest

Being a shlemiel, I listened to every word of every song and weighed them in my head for wisdom. I wanted hints on how to be more like Rick, or Dylan, or David Bowie. After that line about honesty, though, comes an arch, ironic backpedaling, as if the singer doesn't want his song to be a simpleminded battle cry:

I know you always say that you agree

What could *that* mean? (I spent hours wondering about it.) Dylan obviously had just one interpretation in mind, and hated the idea of some *other* person—Marie, for instance—hanging around and not getting it. But what was there not to get? Wasn't it simple? *To live outside the law, you must be honest.* It was the most conspicuous fleck of clear language in the whole swirling mass of melody and noise on those half-dozen albums, and it seemed to sum up the spirit of the noise with a maddening, casual ease.

I hold a grudge against Rick now, but he deserves credit for introducing us to good rock 'n' roll. The first real flashes of musical taste are a kind of self-discovery, and even now I can't overhear anything from *Blonde on Blonde* or *Ziggy Stardust* without remembering how Calaveras Beach felt in the mornings before class that autumn, with the smell of damp pavement and a strong chill in the air evaporating the last traces of summer heat, making the whole town feel as if someone had left a back door standing wide open.

<h1 style="text-align:right">xviii</h1>

On Sunday the phone rang.

"Eric, buddy."

"Hey, Tom."

"Guess where I am?"

"Why?"

"Just guess. Rick called."

"What for? Oh. With a job?"

"Yeah."

"You're at work?"

"Yeah."

"So?"

"So guess."

"How should *I* know? Hi-Fi?"

"No."

"Mr. B's?"

"Dammit!"

"You mean I'm right?"

"I'm behind the counter right now, man. He taught me how to use the register and then just bailed."

"Where'd he go?"

"To Kentucky Fried Chicken. I think he's testing me."

"Testing how?"

"To see if he can trust me." Tom paused. "We had this interview when Rick brought me in today. He said, 'I recognize you,' and started asking questions about my dad. He's a bizarre guy."

"Mr. B?"

"Oh, shit, there he is."

Click.

Soon I felt curious enough to go over. Mr. B's was on the opposite side of the school from where I lived, an easy walk, so I pulled on a windbreaker and left the house. It was a warm day. Over Bartholomew's majestic *B* flapped shrieking pigeons that lived on the roof. I went in, tripping a door chime. Tom and Mr. B looked at me with stuffed, bewildered faces. I caught the breaded smell of Kentucky Fried Chicken and saw a barrel and greasy napkins spread like a picnic on the counter.

"Hey," said Tom.

"Hey."

"Dave, this is my friend Eric."

"Good to meet you," said Bartholomew through his food. He looked sour, but sounded friendly. "Want a drumstick?"

"Sure. Thanks."

I started to eat. Behind them, a little fan turned in the corner without stirring the air. The TV emitted terse dialogue from a Western.

"Rick came in this morning and said how Tom owes money to his asshole friend for dope," Mr. B said suddenly. "You mixed up in that, too?"

"No."

He stared at me with sullen unpleasant eyes.

"Because it's a bad business. Coke's a bad business."

I nodded again. This was my first personal encounter with Bartholomew's foul disposition, and it scared me. His forehead had started to sweat.

"Eric's not involved," Tom assured him. "He had nothing to do with it."

We watched the movie for a few minutes. The fast-food picnic ended with a loud crackling noise from Mr. B, who broke the bone of a chicken thigh with his teeth and sucked at the dark stain of marrow in each half. He did it from habit, like an animal, unaware of being observed. Then he wrapped the wreckage in a napkin on the counter and sat back, satisfied.

"I'm from Kentucky," he said, "and I swear to God I never had fried chicken as bland as that."

"You didn't like it?" asked Tom.

He shrugged and gave a distasteful grimace. "Factory hen."

We went back to watching the movie. Tom glanced up at a truck pulling into the lot. The windshield reflected fierce cold sunlight, and loud heavy metal clashed from the cab. It still beat and thrashed for a few minutes after the motor quit, and in the dimness behind the windshield we could see Harold, Jeremy, and Drew. Jeremy, in the passenger seat, rummaged through the glove compartment, handing cigarettes to his friends. Harold sat behind the wheel with one hairy arm out the window, drumming on the door. Suddenly the doors swung open. I realized I'd never seen Harold's truck up close: It was a primer-grey old Dodge, with square headlights and splotched rear fenders bulging out like a pair of hips.

The door chime sounded. All three kids hesitated at the head of the liquor aisle and stared at us, absorbing the droll information that Tom had a job with Mr. B. They whispered to each other and laughed, then continued down the aisle until Harold found a bottle of Wild Turkey. They drifted toward us, still grinning. Bartholomew's heavy presence muted most of their sarcasm.

At the counter, Harold asked for a pack of Camels.

"Is he old enough?" grumbled Mr. B.

"Are you old enough?" Tom repeated.

Harold gave a weary, wicked smile.

"I think he is," Tom said.

"Card him anyway."

Tom shrugged and turned a smile on the three boys. We both

knew Harold was old enough for cigarettes, but if Tom had to refuse the whiskey, there might be trouble. Harold produced a worn leather wallet that flapped open to show a younger version of himself, a Harold with unshaven hair, on a card with no birth date but a line reading, "AGE: TWENTY-ONE."

"Thanks," Tom said.

The store was silent, except for the TV. Tom rang up their items on the chirping register. When Harold had paid, Mr. B murmured, "Matches," and Tom handed Harold a book of matches.

After a moment, Jeremy blurted, "Are you going out with that chick Rachel?"

"Yeah," Tom said.

Harold gave a slow nod as he unwrapped the cigarettes, but didn't look up. He let his friends do the talking. "Cool," Drew answered, and that was all. It was a neutral visit, accidental but somehow significant, as if the arbiters of manhood at Calaveras High had noticed a troubling shift in Tom's status, which they respected but couldn't bring themselves to trust.

xix

The next Saturday, Tom and I rode to Maui's on a pair of bikes from my garage. Rachel had promised to teach us to surf. ("Maui has a bunch of boards," she'd said. "We can teach you.") No one answered Maui's door, but a note taped among all the stickers read: "Went to 7-Eleven, be right back. ♥ Rachel. Tom was silent. He just turned to sit on one of the brick planters and stared at the stucco houses across the street, where a balding man in a brown suit hurried out to his car.

"Tch," Tom sneered. "That guy looks like Mr. Cantwell."

"Does he?"

"He's got the same twitchy look. Where's he going right now? To work?"

"He's dressed for it."

"On a Saturday?" Tom spat. "Fucking worker bee. Fucking drone!"

"He looks like somebody's boss."

"Even *worse.*"

Tom spat again. His hatred for bosses confused me, since it wasn't connected to any bad experience at Mr. B's. He wore a new pair of mirrored sunglasses and an old T-shirt over jeans that failed to restrain his boxer shorts. The weak winter sunlight warmed us a little. Out of nowhere, Tom said, "I'm gonna paint that Chrysler."

To be sure he was serious, I waited, then cleared my throat.

"What color?"

"Rachel's dad has some blue paint."

"Oh. So he's gonna just *help* you paint the car."

"No, her parents are going away next weekend for some kind of retreat. Rachel says he won't even notice if we use a few cans."

I picked a twig from the planter and snapped it between my fingers. "So you're keeping the car? I mean, this is more than a joke. You're just taking the Chrysler?"

"Why not?"

"What do you mean, why not?"

"You wanna help?"

"You don't need help painting a car."

"Are you scared?"

"No."

"Then what's the problem?"

"I don't want to get involved."

"You're a *pussy.*"

I mustered the sarcasm to answer in a thin voice, "You're such a nonconformist, Tom."

"More than you. I'm an anarchist."

Anarchist! That was news. I ventured, "You don't even know what anarchy means."

"It means no laws. Doing what you want."

"It's a whole philosophy, Tom. It's like a whole way of life."

"*What* philosophy?" He glared at me, hot-eyed. "It's about not *having* any philosophy."

Was this even true? I wasn't sure. Tom sounded well-versed in a subject I hadn't bothered to learn. That was embarrassing, since I got all the good grades.

"So, you can't have a philosophy if you're an anarchist? Is that some kind of rule?"

"You just don't. You live by your instincts."

"You mean like an animal?"

"Like a higher kind of human being. It's not about the brain all the time, Eric. There's a lot more to living than just using your brain."

I was quiet for a while. "—I guess."

"I don't *have* to guess. That's the difference between you and me. I know what I want. I don't have to waste time thinking about it. You let lots of people put their bullshit on you. You're not inner-directed."

"Inner-directed?"

"Yeah."

"You mean anarchy."

"*Total* anarchy. All it means is just not letting other people tell you how to live."

Was *that* true? I had no idea. Tom carried the debate on sheer anarchistic nerve. I snapped another twig and said nothing.

After a minute, Rachel and Maui came from down the street, holding grocery bags. "Hi, hi, hi," said Maui as he let us in, wearing a faded T-shirt and a pair of string-tied pants. He was animated as usual, restless lord of his little red house, offering us fresh orange juice and doughnuts from the store. He and Rachel fussed in the kitchen and spoke in low, intimate voices like fresh-faced lovers on a Saturday morning. Tom didn't seem to notice. He had a funny blind spot about Rachel. His face wore a trusting, calm expression around her that would have been disturbed only if she wasn't there. In any case, Maui kept the atmosphere on an upbeat level that scattered any low suspicion. While we stuffed our mouths with doughnuts and selected boards from his collection, Rachel took a wet suit from the arm of the couch and half-disappeared behind the bathroom door. She dropped her sweats, carelessly, and I felt a bolt of desire at the sight of her bare brown knee.

Then we walked down to the beach. The waves mounded up in solid green swells, curling and flashing in the sun. They were small, but still a problem for beginners like us. I learned that a surfboard can be an awkward vantage point for tackling any size of surf, because it holds you inflexibly face-first into oncoming masses of salt water. The first few waves ran straight up my nose. Rachel showed me how to paddle, and soon I learned to position myself just under the curl of a rising wave and let it carry me forward. That went well enough until the wave bottom dropped and exposed a sucking salty hollow of water and silt. The board's nose pointed down, and I flipped headfirst into the sand. This happened eight times. Meanwhile Maui trotted gleefully on all his waves. Surfing animated him, and his hair collected beads of water which he shook off now and then like a happy Hungarian sheepdog.

Rachel was at home in the water, too, with her slicked-back hair and dark, staring animal eyes. She wasn't as aggressive as Maui, but she could still tear up a wave. The two of them floated a few yards away and spoke in low voices, almost like parents in the front seat of a car, while Tom and I struggled to balance on our boards. Tom crossed his thin arms and shivered, smiling meekly, eyes arched like half-moons. We felt as if a rite of manhood had tasted us and spit us back out. Good local surfers were heroes to us, and I remembered a group of them bobbing in the water one January, during a fierce El Niño winter, when an audience of kids had crowded onto the Calaveras Pier to watch them get killed. The swells had bulked monstrously on the horizon, mounted almost to the level of the pier deck, sprayed our faces and shuddered the pilings, and then toppled in a tremendous crash—these huge, hurricane-radiated freaks of nature, trailing tempests of whitewash. Maui was one of the surfers. He and the rest of those guys could drop feet-first into a twirling sucking valley of water and dance ahead of the curl with a fearless nonchalance, the way other people walk down the street.

After two hours, Tom and I rode our bikes home in defeated silence. We split up on Calaveras Boulevard, and I rode through the streets of my neighborhood feeling drenched with earnest worry. Something about the cold sunlight on the dying lawns outside all the homes left me with the idea that I needed a change. Did I want to end up middle-aged and balding, in an ugly brown suit, rushing to work on a Saturday morning? No! I wanted to be a strong, self-assured individualist, but when I looked inward for a sense of the real Eric Sperling—some shape of a definite person, some overwhelming passion or clear direction—I could find nothing at all.

This feeling came back the next day, when I played Dungeons and Dragons for the last time with the two Dougs. We sat over Cokes and pizza in the Swillinger living room. My character, Captain Morgan, was stranded on a dragon-infested island with his friend Elric, who was Doug Pease's knight, and in one magnificent battle with a band of roving orcs I had cut off eighteen hairy feet and slashed seven thick necks, suffering only a bite on the arm before most of them bled to death in the mud and Doug Pease got up to go to the bathroom.

I knew the courage I gave Captain Morgan in this fantasy game was compensation for a courage I didn't actually feel. Our weekend gaming had started to pale a little. I also couldn't ignore how many books of rules I'd absorbed to play D&D: I had a great talent for learning and living by rules. This idea persecuted me while I chewed on leftover pizza. Tom was right, I thought. I *wasn't* free. All that German guilt, all those Jewish laws! I'd inherited stricture from both sides of the family. Now I wanted to kill the incessant and deep-seated shlemielhood that seemed to live in my belly like a frog, belching up rancid evidence every day that my whole life was running in a wild charge toward college, a wife, a mortgage, a golden retriever, and a station wagon in some child-infested suburb. It was time to do something *now*. I had to take control of my life *now*. I glanced from the dusty upholstered couch we were slumped on to the coffee table, where a paperback with a painting on it like something from India lay unfolded next to an ashtray. The title was *Bhagavad Gita*.

"What are you reading?" I said.

"Oh. That's Hinduism," said Doug. "It's interesting."

I nodded cautiously. Doug Swillinger was versed in ideas I could barely touch; and when he talked about them, I felt myself tense.

"Interesting how?" I said.

He shrugged and settled his head into one bony hand. His eyes glanced up, broad-set and staring in their skewed directions.

"Well, there's this idea of *maya*—the idea that the world is just an illusion," he said. "You know how scientists have figured out that we don't see everything that's in front of us—the world has more detail than our eyes can take in, so our brains have to fill in the blanks. Which means no one can see the world whole, the way it really is. There's a lot we don't even see. So this idea of *maya* says that what we do see is a kind of a dream, shaped by things we want and fear." He glanced down over the rim of his hand at the floor. "It, um . . . it helps with death."

I didn't get it, but I nodded. We rarely talked about his disease. It embarrassed me even to think about. Remotely, I knew Doug had a brilliant mind—shadowy, fate-motivated—but all my efforts to match it faltered. There was a long silence while I thought how tempting it would be to look at the whole cracked, banal surface of Los Angeles County as a layer of stage makeup, a mirage of pavement and plumbing laid against the southern brow of the Mojave Desert. But I couldn't fit my mind around that, and we sat there awkwardly until Doug Pease came out of the bathroom.

XX

Rachel lived in a maze of streets lined with ranch homes and gnarled ash trees. Her driveway connected the street with a detached garage in the backyard, which made the yard a good place for painting a car. Mr. Cisneros had two dozen cans of paint in a toolshed on the rear lawn, and Rachel said he would never miss a few cans because someone had unloaded them all on *him* a year before, and the paint was ugly, an unnatural government blue.

I showed up around eleven. Tom and Rachel were already taping newspaper to the windows. The Chrysler sat on a patch of grass in front of the toolshed. Rachel stacked cans of paint on an oil-stained sheet, and we found a dirty tarp to spread under the car. I felt no guilt, for some reason. A 1976 LeBaron with stale vinyl seats and worn carpeting seemed, all of a sudden, not like a burden or a crime, but like some kind of fabulous gift. We were going to be car owners! Rachel dug an old license plate out of the garage, and it was my job to pry the valid registration tags off the Chrysler's original plate (which we obviously couldn't use) to disguise it. Tom had brought his dad's toolbox and even paid ten bucks for a book on Chrysler maintenance. We smothered the words CALAVERAS HIGH SCHOOL DRIVER TRAINING under two deep coats of gummy latex paint. It went on in thick blue strokes, leaving thin lines that parched in the sun.

Rachel was in a good mood. She wore a faded red T-shirt and smiled through stray patches of paint on her face. She acted like a girl at a lemonade stand or a community car wash—some innocent neighborhood venture—and the free way she touched my arm or flicked me playfully with paint was enough to make me giddy. Meanwhile Tom stalked around the yard with a hard, purposeful, expression. He seemed impatient to get things done.

We finished in a couple of hours and drank glasses of juice, sitting on a couch in Rachel's living room while the paint dried. Her black leather couch sat deep in the dusty-smelling shag carpet. Heavy religious icons hung on the walls, including a foot-high crucifix with bright rivulets of blood in Jesus' hair, and a rounded wooden fish-shape mounted over the TV.

"You said your parents went to a retreat?" I asked.

"Yeah, somewhere down by San Diego. A Catholic retreat."

"They must be pretty religious."

"Yeah. They weren't always. In the sixties, they were these total protesters. They worked for César Chávez."

"What did they do?"

"Everything. Unionized, marched to Sacramento for the grape pickers, got arrested. They make it sound so epic. My dad went to school with César. They squatted in worker camps with him for a couple of years. There was a Filipino camp and a Mexican camp, and it was so fucking Catholic they had to sneak out at night and fool around in the grape fields."

I smiled. "You were conceived in a grape field?"

"I think so. Isn't that funny? But that was in like 1967. Now they're totally Catholic. They won't even *talk* about the grape fields anymore." She stared at the floor and shrugged. "I used to think it was age, but it's really got nothing to do with getting old. They just started to put on a show, like some people do. I think they had to convince somebody they were good, in a certain way."

"Convince who?"

"I don't know, themselves? It's not like they were *bad* before they put all this stuff on the walls. It never made sense to me. I just think it's a show."

Rachel handed us photos of her parents. I saw that her dark round eyes and shameless toothy smile came from her mom, a middle-aged Filipina with threads of white in her hair. Her dad wore ordinary American patterned cotton shirts; he looked slow and well-fed, with a reticent stony face like a Mayan statue. The interest I took in her parents seemed to please Rachel, and we huddled next to each other on the couch. We weren't trying to exclude Tom; he could have been interested, too. But he chose not to be, or else he deeply, truly didn't care. He looked out at the Chrysler and bounced his knee, acting hopped-up with excitement.

"What's the matter?" said Rachel.

"I've gotta fix the ignition," he muttered. "It's felt kind of choppy."

"You're going to work on it now?"

"I wanna get it moving." His eyes flashed. "We've got a car! Isn't that cool? We've got a car to drive."

"You should at least wait till the paint dries."

"It should be dry, shouldn't it? This won't take long, anyway."

He stood up and went out. Rachel and I watched through the sliding glass door while he found his maintenance book in the yard and crawled under the car with a wrench. Drops and patches of blue smeared his jeans. Soon only Tom's legs stuck out from under the chassis; he looked like he'd been run over. For a few minutes in the dusty living room Rachel and I sat in comfortable silence.

I glanced over and noticed a purplish bruise under the crook of her jaw, laid across a thick neck muscle. I hadn't seen it before because of the paint stains on her cheeks; but now, in the cold light from outside, it was hard to miss. Rachel stared back. Her liquid eyes were full of weight and heat. I had the weird idea that kissing her would have been a simple, natural thing to do, but instead, I reached over to brush the bruise with my knuckle.

She ducked away.

"How'd you do that?" I asked.

"Tom did it."

"Excuse me?"

"It's a hickey."

"Oh."

It seemed wrong for a hickey—small but uncontained, spreading like a plum-colored cloud across her slender muscle. But what did I know about hickeys? Rachel gave a curt and guilty laugh. By looking at me with so much feeling, somehow, she'd stripped a varnish from her relationship with Tom, though what was underneath confused me.

I got up to stand at the sliding glass door.

"Hey, Tom? You need any help?"

"I think I got it." In a minute he was on his feet again, blue-smeared but happy. He started collecting his tools. "You wanna go for a ride?"

"Sure."

We cleaned up the backyard and piled into the car. Tom put on his mirrored sunglasses and steered carefully through Calaveras Beach. At first he worried the police would catch us, but after a few minutes he relaxed, rolled down the window, turned on the radio, and settled into the Chrysler's vinyl seat, steering with one hand over the wheel and glaring at other drivers with cool confidence, like Alex in that goddamn film.

Sometimes I like to wonder about my possible futures, about the person I would have turned out to be. Since the accident, my mind has gone on developing, but there's no body or career to go with it. The disconnect leaves a deep riddle. Would I have tried to be a surgeon, really? Eric Sperling in a white coat, stoop-shouldered like his dad, frowning over the results of an old lady's CAT scan in a fluorescent-lit office attached to Cedars-Sinai? I doubt it. A professor is probably closer to the mark, maybe in history or comp. lit., giving classes at a placid Midwestern college overrun by mosquitoes in the summer and dreamy undergraduates in the fall. Or—this is a wild card—I would have migrated to Silicon Valley with Doug Pease, who, according to local gossip, has written a lucrative bit of code and retired at twenty-nine.

Rachel's a lawyer now. From what I hear, she lives in San Francisco with some kind of husband. That's funny, isn't it? Rachel the Gypsy queen, attorney-at-law?

• • •

The morning sun is relentless; Rodney dozes under his hat. Our train rumbles across mud-smelling farmland and sere brush fields south of Bakersfield. The longer I sit here in the sun, the more I remember: I can dig up old memories with a weird clarity, and I want to reminisce about them just like a sparrow wants to sing.

Even under the hot sun I feel like some kind of moon, blinking out and reviving, fluctuating between a sense of human, individual strength and near-total absence. Rabbi Gelanter liked to say that no one could describe what consciousness is—not scientists, not rabbis—and I remember wondering for the first time in his presence why there seemed to be only one creature in the whole history of the world with memories and impressions that I thought of as mine. What if I'd never been born? Where would that sense of self have gone? Who or what would have gotten it instead?

Gelanter also said that *nefesh*, *ruach*, and *neshamah* corresponded to the Christian trinity. There was *neshamah*, he said, the spark of God; then came *ruach*, the connecting spirit (in Hebrew the Holy Spirit was called *ruach ha-kodesh*). And finally there was the suffering human shape.

Even now, in my twilight condition, I can't say I'm religious. My notion of God is a near-total blank. When I think about the faith undergirding everything Gelanter told me I can't imagine how it felt, or what it consisted of. Gelanter was sustained by a sense of purpose and generosity, where I have nothing, or nothing but an urge for revenge.

• • •

A row of telephone poles runs beside the railway. Birds like to sit on the wires in long brown ranks. When the mass of our train thunders by, they scatter into a cloud, full of terror. But these birds are used to trains, and before the monster has even stopped shaking the ground, they settle in scrambled positions along the wire, brownish ranks of bird-bodies basically undisturbed.

xxii

The first game we found for the Chrysler was played in one-way alleys in a part of Calaveras Beach built up with massive, slumbering homes. The alleys ran between the houses and were bordered by walls or chain-link fence. They all ended in deep concrete gutters flanking the broader streets. Tom figured out that if you hit the gutters at full speed, not only did the Chrysler scrape horribly on the pavement, but the car also lurched into the road with a satisfying bounce that sometimes lifted the wheels off the ground. We went out after dinner on Friday nights and prowled these alleys like a thrill-seeking band of wolves. It made me happy to hear the Chrysler engine roar just as the tires slammed into the gulley, to feel the seat float under me so my head grazed the roof, to feel the four wheels bounce on the asphalt while Rachel laughed. The deepest gutters, where they met the alleys, were also dangerously blind, so one of us would sometimes have to stand on the corner and watch for cars while Tom gunned for the trench. Watching from the sidewalk like that was how I saw the Chrysler grind sparks from its front axle and then bound into the street like a frolicking Saint Bernard.

One night, on the way to do gutter jumps, a banged-up Toyota Corolla with a dusty Domino's Pizza sign clamped to the roof passed us on Aviation Boulevard. Tom decided to follow him. Aviation is a thoroughfare running from the L.A. airport along a strip of aerospace buildings. The Domino's driver seemed to notice we were following him. He changed lanes twice, to make sure, then sped forward and suddenly made a hard right, hoping to run away from us up a slope of houses. This grid of houses and shrubs was my neighborhood, not far from the school. Tom swung the heavy Chrysler around the corner and floored the gas pedal. The driver led us through a few mazy turns, right past my house (Tom honked), before shooting onto Aviation again, where we caught him at the next red light.

"Now he's cornered," said Tom.

But the Corolla's door opened, and a pale lanky guy wearing glasses got out with a hammer. He walked up to the driver's side and brandished his weapon. Tom rolled down his window, maybe to keep it from being smashed.

"What's wrong?" he said.

"You guys are following me, and I want you to cut it out."

"We weren't following you."

"Don't pull any shit, okay?" The driver had mouse brown hair and narrow, prismlike glasses. "You're just screwing around, aren't you?"

Tom kept his eye on the hammer. His face had gone pale.

"Fucking cut it out, okay? I've got two hundred dollars on board that car, and I don't need anybody chasing me."

"We weren't after your money."

"Don't even *think* about it," the driver said as he lowered the hammer. "Some of us carry guns."

He stalked back to the car.

"Jesus," said Rachel.

"That was scary," I said.

Tom said nothing; he had turned sheet-white. The light was green for half a minute before he moved again.

Rachel and I sat in the back during these joyrides, like chauffeured passengers, because gutter jumps were best experienced close to the tail of the car. Speeding through the night on a vinyl bench seat beside Rachel Cisneros became one of my favorite activities. We didn't flirt much, but it was still the purest thrill I'd ever experienced, and in a way it was the whole point of hanging out with Tom. He did things that I would never dare. Chasing pizza deliverymen or bounding over a gutter trench in a stolen school car were high adventure, and facing terror like that made me feel scoured clean.

The best ride I remember came one Friday when Tom pissed off the driver of an oncoming pickup truck by yelling, "Asshole!" out the window as it drove by. The truck had been crowding our lane. The driver honked, swerved wide, and started turning around.

"Who is that?" said Rachel. "I recognize that truck."

Tom shrugged.

"Why'd you yell at him?" I said.

"I don't fucking know."

"He's coming after us!" Rachel yelled.

Tom wheeled down a steep narrow street through the tree section and swerved, at the bottom, into a five-road convergence by the railway. Headlights flared in the mirror. Tom turned down a dark frontage road and sped along the tracks. When the pickup gained on us, Tom raised a middle finger at the rearview mirror and leaned on the gas. The Chrysler's engine strained and pulled ahead.

"He's lagging," I said.

The road swerved past some houses and a park. At the intersection with Calaveras Boulevard, barely touching the brake, Tom steered the Chrysler into a wide, high-speed left turn. Our tires chirped.

"Did we lose him?" Tom asked.

"Not sure."

There was a racket of honking and screeching tires behind us. One pair of headlights came speeding out of it, broad-set and square, like a truck's. We were climbing Calaveras Boulevard and losing speed on the hill. The pickup gained on us. In the passenger seat I saw three faces brushed by the slow rhythm of lights overhead. One of them held the passenger door half-open and clutched something in one hand.

"That might be Drew," I said.

"You're kidding," said Tom.

"No, he's right," said Rachel. "It's Harold and them."

"Speed up," I suggested.

"I'm *trying.*"

Harold closed the gap. Rachel and I watched as Drew gripped the dash and leaned out just far enough to whack our sideview mirror with a baseball bat. Compared to the speed of our cars, he acted slow, cool, and methodical. Under the passing streetlights, his face showed no sign of recognizing us. He gave the mirror a single tap, and glass cracked and fell to pieces, one by one, into the onrushing street.

"Jesus," said Tom.

Rachel laughed and grabbed my leg in the dark backseat. Curses came from the truck. Harold and Jeremy flipped us off as they pulled ahead.

I said, "It's amazing who you find just by yelling out your car window."

"Yeah, I wish you'd quit doing that."

The pickup's taillights crested the hill before our Chrysler caught up. Harold and his friends merged into traffic near Pacific Coast Highway, where we lost them in a river of cars. But that was how these outings went. They were like war, or what soldiers say about war—long stretches of boredom broken by flashes of ecstatic terror, lapsing just as suddenly into mundane, tedious night.

xxiii

Soon it was early December. Plastic Santas went up on houses around the city. Mr. B hung lights and some old ropes of tinsel, and storefront windows were sprayed with sticky imitation snow. Winter in Calaveras Beach is cool and damp, with long stretches of desert sunshine, so the town has to fake its Old World traditions in a way I've thought was weird. Why should L.A. try to make its holidays feel like Christmas in London or Stockholm? Jesus wasn't born in some snow-blanketed corner of old Europe. He was born in Palestine, which has a climate like southern California!

Hanukkah was recognized in my house by a dusty electric menorah set up in the living room window by my dad, who seemed to forget about it for a couple of weeks while it shone beside a sparkling Christmas tree. My mom celebrated Christmas with boxes of tinsel and an angel with foil wings. For them the holidays were nostalgic, not religious, and our main celebration was always dinner with the Lindens. Over vegetable dip and crackers we chatted and traded presents; the adults got tipsy and our moms made a production of letting us taste their Gallo wine. In this particular year—the end of 1983, the first holiday spent without her husband—Greta wanted to host, so my parents and I showed up at Windsor Gardens on a Friday evening with a bag of gifts, a platter of stuffed mushrooms, and a cheese log from Hickory Farms. At first, Tom was in a good mood. He wore white jeans and a blue oxford shirt. His fresh haircut made him look more like a sheltered little boy than a young anarchist who'd stolen the school Chrysler and parked it just around the corner.

"Merry Christmas, Eric," piped Greta, dressed in festive purple. I felt awkward in my green wool sweater. The condo had been decorated with plastic holly and mistletoe. That year Tom and I had both asked for surfboards, so I wasn't surprised to see a sleek new orange-and-green board leaning next to the ashless fireplace.

"Hey, I got one, too," I said.

"We should surf tomorrow."

"Sure."

"Come see what else I got."

We went to his room, where an old TV had been set up on his desk. Cascading from the TV were cables for an Atari game on the deep-carpeted floor.

"What games do you have?"

"Adventure and Centipede."

"Cool."

"I also got a Walkman."

Boxes and Styrofoam from the presents were tumbled on his unmade bed. The Walkman lay in a heap with the game cartridges and a bunch of cassette tapes. The clean plaster walls and ceiling were also covered with movie posters: *A Clockwork Orange, Taxi*

Driver, Midnight Express. Tom's room was a place for him to escape his mother into plastic, manufactured dreams.

"Put in Centipede," he said. "You can practice a little. I gotta go to the bathroom."

I snapped the cartridge in and studied the game. Laughter came from the living room. When our parents were together, over wine, it was only a matter of time before the place rang with German women laughing. Thinking about this reminded me of something Rachel had said about her dad's family, who came up from Guadalajara twice a year. "All my aunts laugh like toucans when they're drunk." They were probably laughing that way right now, I thought. Especially around Christmas, the Cisneros house had a darkness that was different from Windsor Gardens, a warm darkness belonging to old L.A. or Mexico—tiny lights on the windows outside like bright strings of confetti, a pale icon of the Virgin Mary lit by votive candles on a table next to the Christmas tree. Rachel's bedroom had a sunburst rug on the floor, a briny wet suit flopped over the back of her chair, and a close odor of surf wax. It was gloomy as well as erotic, and the colored lights shining in from outside were lurid, melancholy, and dim.

Under some laundry on Tom's floor, I noticed the corner of a spiral notebook filled with handwriting. I nudged it free with my foot. The top line started, *FUCKING DEPRESSED, as usual.* A recent date on top. *Rachel & I had another fight.* But before I could read any more I heard Tom flush the toilet, and kicked his notebook back under the pile of dirty socks.

"What are you doing?" Tom said.

"Checking out this game."

"Here, look what else I got. Rick came into Mr. B's and gave me this tape." *Holiday in Cambodia,* by the Dead Kennedys.

"Is it any good?"

"It blows away most of that other stuff he got us."

"Well, put it in."

We listened to it during a game of Centipede. Tom's face grew dream-bound, untroubled. To me the Dead Kennedys sounded flat and dead, like a blast from a gun. But they were supposed to be no-bullshit and cutting-edge, so I kept this opinion to myself.

"You like this stuff?" Tom asked.

"It's not bad."

"I think it completely rocks. Rick said they're playing a show downtown, like next month. I think we should go."

I shrugged. "Sure."

We went on playing. Tom shot and swerved with ferocious energy; he nearly cracked the joystick.

"So how's Rachel?" I said.

"How is she?"

"Yeah, I mean, are you guys getting along?"

"Why wouldn't we be?"

"Tom?" Greta called from the other room. "Eric?" Her voice was piping and cheerful. "Dinner!"

"Shit," I said. He'd thrashed me at Centipede.

"You need practice."

He shut off the Dead Kennedys and we presented ourselves in the living room, where the adults had traded gifts under a low-burning light. Christmas carols played on the stereo; my dad helped Greta pick up wrapping paper. "Don't you boys want your presents?" asked my mom, smiling, with a glass in her hand.

"Ach, they were playing Atari," Greta said. "It's his new favorite toy."

"You'll have to wait now," my dad said, holding a wad of colored paper.

"They can unwrap them after dinner," Greta agreed.

The adults were lightly drunk. In the dining room, Greta had put out candles and silver for a turkey dinner. We sat and said a prayer, then loaded our plates with food. Before we ate, Greta wanted to toast her husband's memory. "As you all know," she said, "Joe can't be with us tonight, so I thought we should drink to him and let him know we're thinking about him. Wherever he might be." She gave a weak smile. My parents murmured something supportive. "To Joe," she said, and everyone answered, "To Joe," and clinked glasses. Tom, though, stared at his plate. The condominium still had that Dri-Erase quality of closeted grief, and fluorescent light from the kitchen had drained the scene of any charm.

"Tom, don't you want to toast your father?" Greta said.

He shook his head.

"*Tom,*" said his mother. "Honestly!"

What he didn't like was Greta's little spectacle; he thought it was phony. He didn't mean any disrespect for his dad. I glanced around for the right gesture to make, something conciliatory and sympathetic, and found a bowl of green beans within easy reach. I cleared my throat and handed them over. It was the wrong gesture, though. Tom hated green beans. He stared at the bowl, and we both noticed the awkward solicitousness in the way I held it out. His eyes went blank with irony.

"What are you doing?"

"Beans?" I said.

"No, I don't want *beans.*"

"Oh."

"*Tom!*" Greta's voice was tight.

Now his eyes welled up. My bumbling had backed him into a corner. He stood, jostling the table, muttered an insult to his mom, and ran for the bathroom. Candle flames quivered.

"Tom, come back here right this minute," Greta called, but the door slammed. Light glowed from behind it, and we heard water running.

"I'm sorry about this," Greta said, and got up from the table.

My parents and I were quiet. My brain shuffled through possible disaster scenarios: Razor blades? Poison? Drugs? The bathroom had a marble sink with broad, gleaming fixtures, a small medicine cabinet, and a cramped shower. I knew the cabinet was almost empty: an old can of Mr. Linden's shaving cream and maybe a jar of Vaseline. Greta kept most of her toilet bleach and painkillers in the master bathroom, which meant that Tom could do nothing worse than waste water through the efficient plumbing. "I've never seen him like this," my mom said to me. "Do you understand it?" I shook my head. We listened to Greta murmur. The faucet ran for a while before we heard a miserably squelched answer from Tom. Then more murmuring. "Just leave me *alone!*" he shouted at last, and his sneaker kicked the hollow door. I heard the inside panel crack like an egg. Soon the door swung inward and Tom appeared, red-faced and hunched, under the soft bathroom light, looking as if he was being tortured by Harold's friends. He whispered something vicious to his mother and bolted for his room.

Greta returned to the table. "I'm really sorry," she said, with a catch in her voice. "But Tom doesn't want any dinner."

"What's the matter?" my mom asked.

"I don't know. He has these spells sometimes."

"He's tired," my dad suggested.

Greta fixed him with her red-rimmed eyes. "He's manic-depressive. That's what the psychiatrist told us."

"You've brought him to a psychiatrist?" said my mom, frowning.

"Yes."

"Since when?"

"Two months now," said Greta. "But it doesn't help with these tantrums."

"Is it drugs, maybe?" my father said, turning his eyes on me. "Do you know anything about this?"

"No."

"Does the psychiatric treatment help?" asked my mom.

Greta shook her head as she gazed at the table. She looked weary now—small-eyed and tired. "I don't think so anymore. No. In fact, I think it's a waste of money."

xxiv

Early the next morning, Tom and I floated on our new boards in the glassy surf beside the pier. The weather was cool, bright, and calm, but the waves were small. We had the beach to ourselves. The sun behind us rose in a grapefruit-colored blaze. Gulls on the pier lights shrieked in mounting crazy voices, and four pelicans glided over the water, touching their wings on the undulating glass, moving their heads in search of fish.

I said, "Last night I heard your mom say you went to a psychiatrist?"

Tom crossed his arms.

"She said that?"

"She mentioned it."

He spat. "I'm not gonna see him anymore."

"Really?"

"He's a waste of time."

"Yeah." I waited for him to elaborate. "That's kind of what she said."

A short sardonic laugh erupted out of him. He squinted at the horizon and tightened his arms. I wanted to ask about Rachel, but I didn't know what to ask or what I thought I would learn. So I said, "Have you seen Harold and them lately?"

"No."

I nodded. "Have they bothered you at all?"

"Like at school? Not in a while." He was quiet, then went on in a surge of raw feeling. "The thing that bugs me is how they still walk around school like they're some big shit, like they're enforcers of the way things are. That's what gets me mad. Like they make the law."

"Right."

"They have to shit on people just to feel good. They need people under them." He shifted on his board and scowled. "And have you noticed how most of the older guys in that crowd, like Ryker, get to be almost preppies in their senior year? They find jobs and come to school all spiffed out, in khakis or whatever, because now they've got to be responsible and they can show everyone how much money they make. Have you noticed that? These guys become *used-car salesmen.*"

"They're idiots, Tom."

He shook his head; he agreed, but I could see his muscles tense with rage under his wet suit. He couldn't relax.

"What's that thing?" he blurted.

"What?"

"Right over there, look."

In the direction of his finger, about thirty yards off, I saw a grey fin arch out of the water. It cruised and sank, leaving a broad, flat, widening ripple.

"Is it a shark?" said Tom.

I didn't think so. "It must be a dolphin."

"How do you tell the difference?"

"Sharks cruise, I think. Dolphins dive in and out."

"Are you *sure?*"

"No."

"Look!"

Tom pointed, and the fin—rubbery, tall, curved, and grey—resurfaced about ten yards ahead. It arched through the water, dark and nicked, with pink sunlight gleaming on the skin.

"I mean, a shark wouldn't keep its fin up *all* the time, right?" said Tom. "Like waving it around, saying, 'Hey, I'm a shark!' "

"I doubt it."

"That's just what you see in the movies. Sharks with their fins above the water. They must show their fins just whenever they feel like being on the surface."

"I guess so."

Tom's forehead wrinkled.

"And don't dolphins move in schools?" he said.

Not a bad point. I scratched my elbow. "I think pods."

"What do you mean, 'pods'?"

"With dolphins it's pods, not schools."

Tom stared for a few seconds in rank incomprehension.

"Jesus fucking Christ, Eric! I can't believe you're correcting my grammar while we're sitting here about to be eaten."

"We're not about to be eaten."

"How do you know?"

"And I corrected your vocabulary, not your grammar."

"Are you out of your *mind?*" Tom's eyes were bright and wild.

"So how come we're sitting here like idiots, if we're about to be eaten?"

"Answer that for yourself, Brainiac!" And Tom paddled for the beach.

Then I was alone. Greenish water flashed; seagulls shrieked from the pier. Light, cool dread seeped into my limbs like a drug. I'd convinced myself it was a dolphin while Tom floated next to me, but with him gone I had trouble making the case to myself.

Far ahead, a wave stirred. I swung around to paddle, snapped to my feet, and noticed the fin riding about three yards behind, sharing the wave. A nervous rush of adrenaline upset my balance and I toppled into the water. My heart kicked in blind panic and for a terrible moment I felt quick razor jaws at my ribs. I jerked once, the way you do in a dream. But nothing really happened. I shook my head free of the water and couldn't see the fin. Tom was laughing on the beach.

"It breathes from its *head!*" he hollered. "It's a dolphin!"

Tom lived for moments like these. He made fun of me by flailing his arms and maniacally rolling his eyes. Later, in front of Rachel, he wouldn't even admit to being scared himself. Exposure as a coward frightened Tom at least as much as any dolphin. When I told her Tom had paddled in to avoid being eaten by a shark, he snapped, "Yeah, but look who fell off his board."

"But *you* paddled in."

"I was going in *any*way, Eric. There were no waves, in case you hadn't noticed. Don't be such a stubborn fuck."

That was how rigid the roles were in our little clan. What Tom had said about Harold's friends was also true about him: He liked to be in charge. He was chief insurrectionist, with me as loyal sidekick, and whenever plain facts threatened to shift our balance of power he would deny them, like any tyrant or bully.

XXV

Our train broils under a noon sun in Bakersfield. The air shimmers, the railyard feels dusty and bleak. We've been here for a while. Rodney stares in my direction with the expression of a baffled sea captain, all searing eyes and bushy, whitening brows.

• • •

Tom's tantrum at the Christmas party reminds me of a series of tantrums he threw in jail after I was killed. He spent the first week of his captivity staring at the cream-painted brick of an isolation cell in juvenile hall. The California Youth Authority Detention Center was literally a hall—or a series of halls—where kids slept in double bunks, but Tom was sequestered in a dim cell of his own because he had misbehaved. His first hours had been a grim process of strip-searching and paperwork, which he endured in silence. The authorities gave him dull-colored sweats to wear and a lower bunk in the hall where other kids annoyed him with questions until he kicked the underside of the bed above him and shouted, "SHUT THE FUCK *UP!*" and they put him in the box for three days.

"The box" had a single aluminum bed and dim fluorescent lighting. Tom lay on his back and watched one bulb flicker through the fly-spotted plastic cover. A public defender interrupted his first afternoon with a consultation to discuss the amount of trouble he was in. Young Mr. O'Connor had wisps of reddish hair retreating across his scalp; he was soft-voiced, blue-eyed, and sympathetic, but also careful to inform Tom that his case would be tough to defend. The worst piece of news was that I had died. If he behaved himself, Mr. O'Connor said, the court just might show mercy. They sat at a wood-grained table in a room painted soothing cream—everything in the detention center was painted soothing cream—and Tom's pupils dilated with bleak fascination at the notion that he was a killer. Now it was official. Eric had died. The prosecutors would pursue a murder charge, but Mr. O'Connor thought their case was weak: He thought they would settle for manslaughter. Tom approached the whole thing with curiosity, rather than remorse. "Sure," he said. "Sure, yeah. I'll behave." And after two days, they took him out of the box and let him roam the hall.

His moods swung violently for a week, until a psychiatrist put him on lithium. Then his emotions calmed and he started making friends. When other kids asked the inevitable question—"What'd you do?"—Tom shrugged and told the same version of the story Mr. O'Connor would tell the court. "I got in a car accident. Some guy died. A friend of mine." He developed a vivid account of something that had never actually occurred. "I guess I was driving too fast, but what happened was, this car rammed into us from the side and we went straight into a truck. Broke the windshield. My friend didn't even have his seat belt on."

"Man, that sucks."

The story took on layers of invented detail, like pearl deposits around a sand particle. Soon it became automatic. Denial wasn't even an issue: Tom never had to deny what happened. He just learned to detour around a certain tar pit in his memory, and retreated to the relative comfort of a psychological prison cell.

• • •

By the time he went to jail, I knew all about Tom's track record with the truth. His self-deceptions were no surprise. If someone had mentioned them to me earlier in the school year, maybe things would have ended better. But dreaming about parallel histories, like I said, is just a waste of time. For anyone else, these weird few months would have been a harmless phase in high school, but for Eric Sperling—this is so *typical!*—they were an overture to disaster.

• • •

Which doesn't mean I've resigned myself to what happened. Fuck what happened! Fuck destiny and fate! Fuck Tom and the whole rotten story of my own demise.

• • •

The train doesn't move.

xxvi

The strangest weekend of the winter came in February, when the Dead Kennedys played a show at the Olympic Auditorium in downtown L.A. It was hot as summer: All week the news had been full of stories about lack of rain and old people dying in rest homes because of a high-pressure system over southern California. On the freeway to the concert, we kept Rick's windows open, and except for the smell of cigarettes in his Impala, we could have been driving, with my parents, to a Dodger game. There was the same anticipation in the car, and even after sundown you felt the same torpid, summery warmth.

The Olympic was a tall, square building in a seedy neighborhood just off the freeway, with GRAND OLYMPIC AUDITORIUM chiseled Roman-style onto vast concrete walls. "They built this thing for boxing matches before the Depression," Rick told us. "I think in the seventies they used it for roller derby." Spotlights shining on the high letters caught yellow strips of some Egyptian-looking design over the door. The whole effect was imperial. We parked in a dim lot behind the hall and waited in line for tickets. The rear of the Olympic was not as grand as the front. A ticket window had three or four chipped and thick-painted wooden frames, and some rear service doors were a dull industrial grey. Kids in leather coats and suspenders milled around, not exactly in line, trying to act like they didn't want to see Jello Biafra.

At the window, as we bought our tickets, a lanky punk with stubble on his head watched money change hands under the wooden frame. "Hey, do you have any change?" he asked, knowing everyone had at least two quarters in change because the tickets cost $12.50. Rick handed over his money. So did Tom. It seemed like the thing to do. I dropped my quarters into the punk's pale hand, but behind me, Rachel said, "Sorry," and kept her quarters. He stared after her and made a sarcastic kissing sound.

"Shut *up*," Rachel said. "God!"

"He's probably a junkie," Rick informed us on the way in. "You can't argue with them."

The Olympic had two levels of seats arranged around a pit. We sat on the upstairs level behind an iron rail. Smoke from joints and cigarettes rose like a fog and swirled in the empty middle of the hall, above the stage. A drum kit waited between two black wings of amplifiers. Rick said it was the Dead Kennedys' drum set, and that from the look of things we'd missed the opening band. "No big loss," he said. I didn't mind. I glanced around at the crowd. The people made the patrons of The Garage look timid: There was hair in long spikes dyed blood-red at the tips; there were tremendous mohawks on polished heads; women wore negligees under their leather coats or just T-shirts with the sleeves torn off that half-exposed their breasts. People wandered up and down the aisles, sometimes in a hurry, as if they had urgent business in another part of the hall. *Doctrine, society, law*, I thought. It was intimidating. All I had on was a thin plaid shirt handed down from my dad, and sneakers.

Suddenly the hall went dark, and a roar went up like wind in a tunnel. The damaging guitar started, then the nervous drums. When the lights came up a deep shade of green, we could see the band moving around like men on the floor of an aquarium. Jello Biafra had a crazed, whining voice. After a few minutes it seemed to find a corner of my brain to aggravate, the way a baby's cry is supposed to addle the brain of a parent. The crowd began to move. A slam pit opened in front of the stage, and the raucous noncon-formism in the Olympic melted—under the noise and presence of the band—into a kind of mob rule.

During the first set of songs, I stole glances at Rachel. She wore sneakers, jeans, and a faded red T-shirt that hung from her breasts like a thin curtain. She smiled at me. I smiled back.

"Tom says he wants to go downstairs and slam," she said.

"Okay," I said, just to be agreeable, and we smiled again.

But nobody moved.

During the next song, I felt a hot flare of smoke against my ear, as if Rachel had lit a cigarette, but Rachel was watching the band. A rolled-up tube of newspaper, held by a drowsy kid in the row behind ours, was leaking smoke. He'd rolled it for the special purpose of blowing smoke between our faces. I felt caught out, somehow, as if this kid—who was just stoned and acting strange—had noticed me smiling at Rachel and could somehow tell she wasn't my girlfriend. In the light from the stage, I saw his pale face staring down along the tube. He wore limp dreadlocks and an army-green jacket. "That's real funny!" Rachel shouted at him, but the kid didn't answer, he just kept blowing smoke. Finally I grabbed the paper tube and flung it over the rail.

"How come you had to do that, man?" he started to yell. "How come you had to *do* that?" His voice was thin, maybe from smoking pot. He moved up to the railing beside me. His face looked blurry, distracted. He swung his arms like some of the kids in the slam pit; now and then he shouldered into me.

"What's he doing?" Rachel said.

"I'm not sure."

The kid knocked into me again.

"I think he wants to slam-dance up here against the railing."

Rachel watched him. Then she asked, "Are you having fun?"

"Not really."

The kid lurched into me one more time. I pushed him away, but he grabbed my arms and started to pull. This took me by surprise. He yanked me into the aisle, where we both fell onto the stone steps. Rachel, and then Tom, tried to pull him off, but by then a pair of huge men in polo shirts and belted pants were already coming down the steps. Tom started to say, "It was this guy, man, it wasn't him."

But the bouncer who grabbed me said, "No slamming on the top floor. That's the rule," and pulled me by the scruff of the shirt up the stairs to the pale-yellow concourse.

They dumped us both in the parking lot. Rachel came out, too. The kid looked at her and swayed a little on his feet. Then—without looking at me again—he said, "Shit!" and walked off toward the sidewalk.

"That was weird," said Rachel, watching him go. I sat down against the wall. "Are you hurt?"

"I think I bruised my shoulder on the stairs."

She squatted next to me and touched my shoulder. Her eyes looked lively, excited. I noticed a tiny drop of blood at the edge of her lips.

"Hey, you're bleeding."

"Am I?" Rachel laughed and wiped away the blood. "That kid hit my face."

"Doesn't it hurt?"

"Nah."

Another bead of blood appeared, glistening in the streetlight. I wiped it away with one finger. Our faces were about six inches apart. I brushed her bangs from her eyes, and she smiled. All the mayhem of the last few minutes collected into a single electric thrill along my spine. Did she want me to kiss her, really? Why else was she crouching so close? I smiled back, and finally, without thinking about it—this may have been the most spontaneous thing I'd ever done—I leaned up and caught her lips with mine. She put one hand on my arm to steady herself, but didn't pull away. Her mouth felt thick and soft.

When we finished, she chuckled.

"You taste salty," I said.

"That's the blood."

She wiped her mouth and laughed. A bright, bluish dandelion of light radiated from a building across the street.

"I wonder where Tom and Rick are," she said suddenly, standing. "They were gonna follow me out."

Her mood was different. She put her hands in her pockets and looked at the door, as if nothing had happened. My mood changed just as quickly. I decided that kissing her had been a mistake. For Rachel it was just a joke, a little game, so for me it would be too.

"*There* he is!" Tom's voice rang from the doorway. Rick was behind him. "Fucking Sperling, man. Leave it to him to get kicked out of a Dead Kennedys concert."

"What did that guy want from you?" Rick said.

"I'm not sure. I think he was just stoned."

Tom put his arm around Rachel's waist. I watched her kiss him.

"Well, what should we do now?" said Rick.

"Will they let you back in?" said Tom.

"The bouncer said I shouldn't even try."

"I kind of want to go somewhere else," Rachel said, turning to Rick. "Didn't you say something about Dockweiler?"

On the way to the concert, Rick had told us about bonfire parties on Dockweiler Beach, just north of Calaveras, beyond a massive oil refinery. "They've been happening ever since I was in high school," he said. "Good place to go, when the weather cooperates."

Rachel shrugged. "Let's go there."

"Okay."

"Sure."

"Why not."

Pacific Avenue ran along the top of a cliff near the refinery. In the dark you looked down from the road into the tubes and orange-lit industrial mist. Farther on, you parked by the curb and followed a long wooden staircase down to the beach. By nine o'clock every Friday, a pile of supermarket pallets was set blazing on the sand, while kids in flannel shirts and gang members with bandannas sat drinking forty-ounce beers. We settled on a wooden landing at the base of the steps, where water from a drainage pipe created a marshy riverhead and a dirty stream to the surf. Rick sat forward on the stair landing and passed around a bottle of Smirnoff from the trunk of his car. He watched us with his narrow, intelligent eyes. "So at the show Tom said something about driving around on weekends. You guys are driving now?"

"Tom has a car," said Rachel.

"Oh, yeah?" Rick smiled. "Christmas present?"

"It's a driver-training car."

Rick wrinkled his forehead. "Oh. You went to an auction or something?"

"No," I said lightly. "He took it."

"Shut up."

"He's serious," said Rachel.

"You're driving around a stolen school car?"

"Sure," Tom said. "I mean, we painted it. It doesn't look like a school car."

Rick smiled and shook his head. He kept smiling, not sure how to react. "You're insane," he said quietly. "We never did anything like that." He stared at the sand and his face changed color. I thought he was about to give a speech. I figured he would tell us the car was taxpayer property and that we had stolen a public resource without thinking of all the kids who would never learn to drive. I was ready to feel profound, stabbing guilt. In fact, I felt guilty anyway. But Rick said, "Once my friends and I stole a canoe at Disneyland. You know those canoes you can paddle? We shoved our Disneyland guide in the water and took off by ourselves. It took 'em three hours to catch up with us in that kind of lagoon they have." He snickered. "We spent the night in jail."

Tom reclined cockily. "But you never stole a car or anything like that?"

"No, we never—I guess"—Rick slung his arms around his knees and looked thoughtful—"I mean I don't think it's *wrong* to steal from the System, you know. We just never made a point of it."

Tom took this as a deep compliment. I'd never thought of stealing the Chrysler as a political statement, but he didn't seem to mind. Beyond his head, and Rick's, I could see the bonfire throwing sparks. The vodka confused me and I lost the thread of conversation.

Rachel leaned over and plucked the sleeve of Rick's T-shirt, to look at his tattoos. "Who's *Anna?*" she asked.

"She was an ex-girlfriend. Actually that was my first tattoo."

"Let's see," said Tom.

Rick held his arm out and we saw the name ANNA in faded block letters, written above a more professional tattoo, a ring of leaves girdling his thin muscles.

"That's sweet," Rachel said.

"Yeah, real sweet." He grimaced. "I scarred myself trying to get rid of it."

Rachel poked at the skin. "Is that why it's all puffy?"

"I tried to burn it off."

"*That* must have hurt." But Rachel chuckled. She wore a curious, mischievous smile. "Were you gonna marry her?"

"Me, get married?" Rick shook his head, pulled from the vodka, and smirked. "I thought it would last more than six months, though."

"How come you wouldn't get married?" Tom asked.

Rick was silent for a while. "It's kind of scary, don't you think? A few of my friends were happy just living together until they decided to get married."

"Why?" said Rachel.

"I think it's because the whole point of marriage is respectability. People get married 'cause they think they should. It's just a bourgeois tradition—this respectable way of presenting yourself to the world. I think that's a strain."

We nodded. His voice was low, meditative, but it carried over the noise of people coming down the creaking stairs.

"It's like college," he said. "Everyone I fucking knew in high school went to college. I mean, that's just not necessary. It has nothing to do with scholarship or education. College has turned into a finishing school for the middle class."

He scratched his shoulder, and Rachel lit a joint. Sweet, thick smoke flared up and she passed it around. Rick circulated the vodka.

"Real education doesn't come from a degree, anyway," he said.

"Where does it come from?" I asked, and Rick glanced up, surprised.

"It's just . . . experience. *Life*. A degree's nothing but a label to place you in society, like a big stamp on your head. A great, big Establishment stamp," he said with rising emotion, "that people who believe what they see on TV use to judge you by." He shook his head. In the orange shine that reached us from the flames and from the lights on the road above, I saw his face twitch angrily. He shouted, "I am so *sick* of getting asked where I went to college! You can feel people trying to pin you down, when they ask you that. Trying to *place* you." He spat on the sand. "Once I had a guy skip the first question altogether, and ask what my *grade point average* in college was. Like it was some kind of competition."

We listened like initiates while Rick went on about Society, the System, and capitalism. He was alienated by American life the way we were alienated at school, and his sweeping disaffection was seductive. It had evolved from simple rebellion into an apparently moral way to live, and none of us had been exposed to much moral direction before. He told us that yuppie conformism was a dangerous descendant of the bourgeois social order, dangerous because Hitler had exploited bourgeois complacency in Germany. The American Revolution itself had been a bourgeois revolution—not like the one that was coming—and an ethic of late-bourgeois conformism was going to wreck this country's freedoms. Consumerism. The Cold War. The military-industrial complex. Television, Hollywood, the network news. Rick ran through the arguments like reading a script. But they were new to me, and I felt ashamed for acting so weak-willed compared to Tom. A few years earlier, it had dawned on me that everything on TV wasn't true or even any good, but it was Rick who focused my thinking on shadowy and near-invisible structures of power, so that where I once saw frightening news stories, uproarious comedies, tear-jerking family dramas, and charming cartoons, now, sometimes in the same programs, I started to see an electromagnetic wasteland of media power, storms of influence raging across the American desert looking for the most weakly rooted forms of life to give up votes and money and admiration and time.

Rick's idealism was bracing because of its heroic dimensions—he sketched a vague network of technocrats and corporate managers and politicians who needed to be brought down—but he also turned ordinary teenage contrariness into a political pose, meaning that Tom's courage with the Chrysler, to him, was more than just a high-school prank. He called Jello Biafra an "underappreciated politician." He spoke in dark tones about Reagan. He hated Christians, but quoted Emerson—" 'Whoever wants to be a man must also be a nonconformist' "—and by the end of his speech, I wished vividly and devoutly that *I* had stolen a car.

We sat cross-legged on the sand, with the fire burning behind us. Rick sat on the wooden edge of the staircase as he talked, and Rachel was close enough to grab his leg flirtatiously now and then. Her eyes began to shine. The vodka had kicked in, and her sense of boundaries blurred. She crawled around whispering things into Rick's ear, or into mine, and then fell laughing in the sand. Tom didn't react. Maybe the alcohol made him recede socially, as much as it expanded Rachel. But hints of her faithlessness also bounced off him like rocks off the side of a house. He stared at the cliff while she lay on her back and gazed at the stars. I focused on the sound of water trickling from the drainpipe.

"We should have beer or something to cut this stuff," Rick said, holding his vodka up to the firelight. "Anyone want beer?"

"Where would we get it?"

"Playa del Rey's right up the highway. Practically at the top of the stairs."

I didn't remember any store on the highway, but Tom said, "Sure, if it won't take too long."

"Shouldn't. Wanna come?" Tom nodded and got to his feet. "We'll be right back," Rick said.

"Okay."

They mounted the wooden stairs and disappeared, into the glare of streetlights from the highway. Rachel sat with her back against the landing, drawing in the sand with one finger. I thought about our kiss outside the Olympic. I didn't want to start another awkward situation like that, so I stood up.

"I have to pee."

She stared up at me. "You do?"

The trickle of water was torturing my bladder. "Yeah. Pretty bad."

She shrugged and went on drawing in the sand. I'd never seen Rachel drunk before.

"So I'll be right back."

"Okay," she said.

I staggered off to a private corner of the cliff base beyond the stairs. The bonfire raged in the middle of the beach. Tall flames licked up behind a crowd of people, and a cloud of heavy smoke lingered and folded in layers over their heads, bottom-lit as it floated into the sky. I turned to undo my pants. The cliffs glowed with a shifting orange light. At first the only sounds came from the fire and the churning surf. But I still hadn't started to pee when I heard Rachel's voice calling my name.

"Oh," I said. "Hi."

"What's the matter, won't it come out?"

"Not yet."

She stepped past me, to the foot of the cliff, where the shadows obscured part of her body. She pulled down her jeans.

"You mind if I go?" she said.

"I guess not."

She gave one of her curt, throaty laughs. Firelight touched her rump and I could hear the stream drill into the sand. She bent her head like a little girl to watch it, then pulled on her jeans and came over to me.

"Still nothing?"

I shook my head.

"I'm a little shy sometimes," I said.

"Huh. I've *noticed.*"

She lingered so close that one of her hands touched my arm. Her breath stank of vodka. "Maybe you need help?" she asked, and rested her chin on my shoulder.

"I—"

Shouts came from the fire. The mixture of alcohol, lust, and fear almost made me fall over.

"What are you doing?" I whispered, but she just chuckled again and clicked her tongue. What she was doing was gently stroking my forearm with her fingertips.

"Where's Tom?" I said.

"*I* don't know. Up on the road, with Rick."

Her voice was light and bated. My heart slammed. For a few minutes I felt only desire, salt air on my skin and the soft pressure of her chest against my arm.

She looked down, over my shoulder, and gave another grunting laugh.

"There's probably no hope now."

"I guess not."

My dick stretched up from the shadow of my hips into the flamy light.

"You should lie down," Rachel suggested. A bend in the cliff face gave us some privacy. The moon hung vivid and bright overhead and we heard a clamor of shouts from the bonfire. Her lips, when she kissed me, felt salty and wet, obscene, like a mussel or a clam.

The whole mob of drunken kids had started to moil and sway. Rick had told us it was normal for brawls to break out near the fire—he said someone usually got stabbed before the cops arrived—and sure enough, while Rachel and I watched from the shadows, the crowd melted into a seething mass, flannel shirts swaying and bottles flashing in the firelight, violent racket swelling as people folded into the brawl and the crush of bodies started to drift across the sand. It was just like water boiling. The mob percolated at first, a few surges of violence, then spilled out in a long and senseless roil of bodies bucking for blood.

"I don't think it's safe to be here," I whispered to Rachel.

"Of course it isn't *safe*," she said with a crooked smile; and, still smiling, careless and drunk, she reached back to hold me with her lovely slender fingers and sank her tender body onto mine.

part four

xxvii

"When a man is aroused to mate with his wife," reads the Zohar, "all parts of the body agree on this and are prepared to receive enjoyment from it. Then the *nefesh* and the desire of the person indulge willingly in that act."

I've got my book back from Rodney. He fell asleep in the grain and I took it out of his backpack. Not everyone understands what a steamy document the Zohar can be. The *nefeshot* spend their days and nights lusting after the living, having sex in dreams, disrobing, and appearing in visions to their widowed spouses. Purgatory must have been a boisterous place for medieval Jews, or at least more sexed-up than it is for me.

As for what I did with Rachel, my only defense comes from the Zohar: All parts of the body and soul agreed.

xxviii

"Greetings," Doug Pease said to me at lunch on Monday after the bonfire.

"Hey, guys," I said.

"Tom found some other friends?"

"I don't know. He's acting funny."

"I like his new hat."

"Yeah."

From our spot on the grass we watched Tom eat french fries from a paper tray. Spending time with Rick had given him permission to look more wired and ragged at school. Now he wore not just aviator sunglasses and overflowing boxer shorts, but also a woven Mexican cowboy hat that looked menacing tilted low on his apple-smooth face. This costume sent an obscure signal to the other students. They noticed him now: His lawless posture stood out against the background of Calaveras High in bright relief, like an Egon Schiele figure against a Hockney painting.

"Who's that with him?" said Doug Pease.

"I think Robin Lansing."

"Since when are *they* friends?"

"I don't know."

Robin sat next to Tom under hedges of oleander at one end of the cinder-block wall. He was our sophomore class president. If Tom was learning to dress like a rebel, Robin put himself forward as a promising young politician. He brought books on Wall Street to class, cultivated friends in every clique, and worked with Chuan in a campus cocaine ring. His skinny neck stretched like a turtle's away from bent shoulders, and he wore rimless glasses, like the corporate lawyer he would grow up to be. His manner was curious, relaxed. *What's this guy's story?* he seemed to want to know, sitting next to Tom. *Where's he coming from?* He adjusted his glasses while they talked, crossed his arms, and squinted cannily across the yard.

At the end of their conversation, Tom handed Robin a brown paper bag.

"You do anything good last weekend?" Doug Pease asked. "You and Tom chop down any more trees?"

He wore a smug, froglike smile.

"I had sex with Rachel."

"Shut up!"

"I did. I had sex with Rachel Cisneros."

Doug Swillinger turned his head and looked at me with one stray eye.

"Is that why you're not sitting with Tom?"

"Yeah, does he know?" Doug Pease said.

"I haven't told him."

Robin got up to leave, and Rachel sat down on the cinder-block wall with a slice of greasy pizza from the cafeteria. Behind her, to the right of the oleander, grew a row of naked rosebushes. She didn't look at Tom. He was talking to her, but she just gazed at her pizza and chewed. They acted this way a lot, in private. I had seen it before. After four months of going out, Rachel and Tom had lapsed already into the strange, slow rhythms of a marriage.

"So what's it like?" Doug Pease asked.

I was distracted. "What's what like?"

"Losing your *virginity.*"

I'd been dwelling on this continuously since the bonfire, of course, but coming from Doug it seemed like a stupid question.

"Hard to describe." I tore up grass beside my shoe. "You have to experience it for yourself."

"That's a lame answer."

"Well, sorry."

I stretched on the grass and yawned. The truth was, I didn't feel much different. The weekend was a dark blur, and compared to the shattering Dead Kennedys show, or the dissolute hours by the bonfire—laced with Rick's politics—the act of sex seemed not exactly life-changing. I was a little disappointed. How could something you fantasize about for years turn out to feel so . . . normal? And it was all over now. Had been over for days. That was the other surprise. Sex didn't even last as long as most pop songs about it.

Still, Rachel and I traded smiles in the schoolyard and sometimes talked by ourselves in the locker hall. We avoided real conversation: Rachel would tell me about her noisy aunts, or her English homework; I talked about math tests and surfing. She laughed at my jokes in distracted little bursts, as if what I said wasn't really the point; her eyes tried to read my face for clues to how I felt. How I felt was fond, tender, shy, and scared. I thought about her constantly. But I didn't want to impose myself, because what if she thought having sex with me had been a mistake? We'd both been drunk. What if she regretted it? There was a newly dyed streak of blond in her bangs, and the glimpses of brown skin and black eyes I caught behind it were pained and melancholy. Sometimes she seemed anxious to tell me a secret.

One day, while Tom sat with her on the wall, I went up to ask a question. Tom leaned forward with a bag of potato chips and studied the campus through his sunglasses, bouncing his knee nervously. I said hi; Rachel smiled. Tom just crunched his chips.

"What are those packages Robin gets from you?" I asked.

He stopped chewing. "What do you mean?"

"You give him packages of something. Brown bags. I've seen it three times now."

"So?"

"So what's in them?"

He swallowed his chips and stared across the yard. Kids sat in clusters on patches of grass, outside classroom doors, under the shade of concrete overhangs.

"I'm selling him some of Miles's coke."

"Oh."

I looked at Rachel. She gazed at her feet.

"*That's* a good idea," I added.

"Whaddayou mean?"

I shook my head.

"I got a bag from him right now," he said.

"From Miles?"

"Look."

Tom opened his backpack, then reached in to rustle a paper bag, and I saw the corner of a Ziploc package of white powder.

"He just gave you that?" I said.

"He gave me a bunch, and said if I sold it all, and kicked back enough of the money, we'd be clear."

"When was this?"

"Right after the bonfire."

"And Miles trusts you?"

Tom shrugged. "Rick said he'd vouch for me."

We were quiet for a minute. I was confused and slightly nervous. Then he said, "Wanna try some?"

"No. We can't, can we? You need it all."

"Not all of it. Miles said I can keep whatever I make over what I owe him. There's a lot here."

He looked at me with his mirrored sunglasses. I felt conflicted. Part of me wanted to impress Rachel. Another part hated the idea of inhaling something that looked so much like chalk dust. Cocaine belonged in dance clubs and films about rich people, not in Eric Sperling's nose. But this was another chance to step outside myself and become something besides a shlemiel; so at last I said, "All right, well, let's hurry," and we retreated to the boys' bathroom before the bell rang.

xxix

Rachel came with us. The bathroom was unmonitored. In fact, it was just a desolate space of pale blue tile between the quad and locker hall that no one used for a bathroom because the stall doors had all been stolen. A thin layer of slime covered the tiles. Graffiti in black marker said SABBATH RULES, and a few dried patches of toilet paper mulch clung to the ceiling. We stood in one corner by the urinals, under a grated window that let in hot bright sun.

The first thing Rachel did in the bathroom was step up to a urinal and drop her pants. She bent her knees a little and pissed straight at the porcelain, like a boy.

"Hey," I said. "Girls can't do that."

"*Some* girls can."

I gazed at her broad brown rear end curving beneath her flannel shirt. Across the back of one thigh there was a faded purplish bruise, like a large mottled cloud below her skin. I was shocked by the size of it, but she hitched up her pants without saying a word or glancing at me. Tom pulled out the cocaine, a pack of cards, and the carefully sawn hull of a ballpoint pen. On a shelf in front of a busted wall mirror he arranged three lines on the card pack. He offered it to Rachel; she leaned her head in and snorted.

Then Tom offered it to me. I said, "Go ahead," because I still felt stiff with fear. Soon Tom was making snuffling noises. He rubbed the sides of his nose and half-closed his eyes just to handle the Intense Inner Experience as the drug slapped the base of his brain.

"What happened to your leg?" I asked Rachel, heart pounding.

"What do you mean?" Rachel said. "Oh. The bruise. That's from skateboarding."

Tom handed me the pack of cards and the pen segment. In a quick sniff, I inhaled the bitter dust, which caked at the back of my sinuses and began to tingle. To pull the wet goop down my throat, I swallowed—hard—wiped my nostrils, and closed my eyes. Nothing. At least, not at first. Then we heard voices in the hall. The door creaked open and Ryker, Jeremy, Harold, and Drew came in chattering. They saw us, paused, went silent, and looked as surprised as they had at Mr. B's, taking in one more bit of droll information about Tom Linden and his friends. Tom stuffed the drug paraphernalia into his backpack, not quite in time. Harold laughed and widened his eyes.

"Whaddaya got?" he said.

"Nothing."

With a slow, easy smile, Harold moved to the sink to wash his hands. He had a knack for establishing control. We watched him rub his hands under the trickle of water and frown at his ruddy, stubbled face. He shook his hands dry, because the paper-towel dispensers were empty. Then he approached Tom slowly and circled him.

"I asked you what you *had*."

"It's none of your business what I have."

Harold stared at him crazily, the way he'd stared at us both in the Swamp. His patience was gone. After staring at Tom for a while, he decided to knock off his hat.

"Cowboy? Huh?" he whispered.

"*Urban* cowboy," Ryker suggested.

"John Travolta," Drew elaborated.

"Fucking *faggot*," Jeremy said in a half-whisper, pulling their train of thought around to its usual station.

We heard more voices in the hall, adult voices this time, as well as the rubber scrape of a dragging tennis shoe I had learned to associate with Larry the narc. We turned to see Larry's head pop through the door—eyebrows raised, half-smiling—and he said, "Hey!" He shuffled in, followed by Greg, his partner. "I thought I heard something in here. What's going on?" Smiles, to cover serious, penetrating eyes. Tom and Rachel looked clean, but I wasn't absolutely sure there wasn't a streak of dust on my upper lip. My heart beat furiously. Greg's uptilted face inspected mine. To clean whatever traces of coke might be stuck to my nostrils, I wiped my nose vigorously, and sneezed.

"What are you guys doing?" he asked.

"Just washing our hands," Tom said.

I took this cue and went to the sink. I sneezed again. My sinuses and throat felt numb.

Larry faced Rachel. "This is the wrong bathroom for you, isn't it?"

"He had to wash his hands. I just followed him in. It's no big *deal.*"

I felt the first onrush of glassy pleasure from the drug, and sneezed again. This time a spray of blood moistened the porcelain sink. My brain felt crystalline, bright. I ran more water and wiped my nose, but that just encouraged the blood to slide out in a diluted sheet across my upper lip. In the cracked mirror I looked like something from a horror movie. (Why couldn't I misbehave gracefully?)

"Are you okay?" Greg said, moving to help me with a paper towel.

"Just a nosebleed."

"We better get him to the nurse's office," said Larry.

"Come on. You okay?" Greg asked.

I nodded. He led me into the locker hall. I was holding a bloody paper towel to my face. My heart beat like a hummingbird. I felt exhilarated, panicked, and dazed. The banks of metal lockers and the stone floor in the hall—not to mention the office building with its concrete overhang, propped by beige-painted poles—all had a vibrant fluttering beauty I had never noticed before. I seemed to slip between sheets of crystal in the air and even smashed through them, painlessly, victoriously, while other kids slouched or trudged pathetically back to class. When Greg presented me to the dour, bent-shouldered, cabbage-haired woman with half-glasses who was our school nurse, Mrs. Schneider, I also had a hard-on.

"Hi, Mrs. Schneider, we have a nosebleed case for you."

"Oh, dear. What happened?"

"It wasn't a fight or anything. He was in the bathroom, and he started to sneeze. Then his nose started to bleed."

"Well, put him on the couch."

They stretched me on the coarse brownish couch at one end of the windowless office. Then Greg left and Mrs. Schneider asked, "What's your name?"

"Eric Alan Sperling."

"Do you have a cold?"

"I don't think so."

"What about allergies? Are you allergic to pollen?"

"Dogs."

"You're allergic to dogs?"

I nodded. It seemed like an interesting question. "We had a puppy once, Petey? Who I was allergic to. But just for the first month we had him, because I got over it in a month and my dad said I'd built a resistance to his fur. He died in an accident with a car. Petey did. That was four years ago. So maybe the resistance is gone. I don't really know."

"Was there a dog in the boys' bathroom?"

"Not that I saw."

"Put your head back."

She covered me with a thin blanket and handed me a fresh paper towel for stanching the flow of blood from my nose. When it stopped, she offered water in a paper cup.

"Feeling better?"

"I feel amazing."

"What's your fifth-period class?"

"Trigonometry with Mr. Dowd."

She wrote me a re-admit. I arrived in trig ten minutes late, still hard beneath my jeans, and waved at the teacher as I sat behind my desk. I had tried to be quiet, unobtrusive, but Mr. Dowd stared at me balefully. I felt bright and strong. For the first half-hour, I peppered Nicola with notes until Mr. Dowd ripped one of them from my hand and tossed it into the wastebasket. Then I put my head down and felt the first glimmer of a powerful headache. By the end of class I was dejected, tired, and oppressed by a throbbing in my skull. I decided to ditch sixth period and go to bed. I also decided that my cocaine days were *over*—only an hour after they'd begun— and felt too weary to care whether Larry or Greg saw me leaving school.

XXX

Around three, lying in bed, I heard the gate to our front yard open. People who knew us never used the front gate; they knocked on a pair of flimsy French doors that opened onto our deck. I figured it was a salesman. Our house was built on a slope, and the front door stood high enough to justify a tall porch with a flight of steps. These steps were enclosed by a stucco wall that slanted in front of my window. Anyone on the steps could look into my room, if they wanted, so to keep the salesman from seeing me, I hunched in one corner of the bed, wrapped my knees with both arms, and held my breath, trying not to make noise. My head throbbed. I felt too rotten to face any strangers.

A girl's voice said, "Eric. You in there?"

"Rachel?"

"Hey."

Her streaked hair and round eyes showed above the windowsill. I also saw the shoulders of her zippered cotton sweatshirt and the *pukka* shells on her neck.

"Come on, I'll let you in."

At the entryway, Rachel had to step over boxes of old paperwork my dad had piled against the wall. The light switch at this end of the hall was broken, which gave our entryway the look and shape of a closet. Dad used it as one.

"Sorry, we kind of ignore the front door. You've never been here, have you?"

"Never inside."

She stood half-smiling in the dusty hall. My head throbbed, but I realized as we stood so close that it wasn't just Rachel who had never been inside the house: An actual teenage girl was an unknown phenomenon at the Sperlings'.

"Well, I'll give you a tour. You want some juice or something?"

"Sure."

"Come on."

In the kitchen I poured two glasses of cranberry juice, then showed her the living room, the dining room, and my bedroom. She took it all in with silent black eyes, sipping from her glass.

When I finished, all she said was, "So how do you feel after that stuff Tom gave us?"

"Pretty bad. I came home early."

"I figured you did, when I didn't see you after class." She gave a tight, ambiguous smile. "It was strong coke."

She stared from beneath her bangs, and stood closer than she ever allowed herself to stand at school; the slight warmth from her body stirred me. When I returned her stare she didn't glance away, so I touched her elbow, set down my juice, and kissed her.

The secret to Rachel was that she was unsentimental about sex: She didn't fall for boys the way I was falling for her. She was a tomboy who liked to experiment with her own new powers of seduction. When she took off her clothes that afternoon, I noticed a half-dozen bruises on her torso and hips. I was shocked again, but didn't ask about them, because I knew Rachel had been getting into fights and falling off skateboards since about the age of five. The world didn't exist for her unless she could knock into it, feel it with her muscles and limbs. After puberty, she brought the same reckless attitude to sex. She'd grown up on local elementary-

and middle-school playgrounds like the rest of Calaveras High, and she was accepted; but Rachel was also too much of a hoyden to deal with the gentle, shifting confederacies of white girls, and too much of a flirt to keep away from boys. I was learning that she collected boys like bug specimens. She flirted and fucked just to see how we behaved.

Afterwards I said, "Does Tom know anything about us? I mean, at Dockweiler?"

She shook her head.

"You haven't told him?"

"No. He gets jealous enough as it is."

This came as a surprise. "He doesn't seem that jealous."

"I know, he hides it pretty well. He doesn't want you to think he gets jealous of you. He gets jealous of all the time we spend together, the three of us."

"I had no idea."

"If Tom had his way, it would just be like me and him in some cave." She laughed. "He needs a lot of attention."

I nodded.

"You know what I mean?"

"I'm not sure."

"He's like a little boy. He gets jealous and needy. He throws tantrums."

"Oh. Sure."

"Almost as soon as we met, he glommed on to me. We were quote 'going out' before I knew about it. Right after Maui's party, we were like boyfriend and girlfriend. Up till then I thought I was in kind of a no-boyfriend phase, where I wouldn't go out with any one person, but Tom needs to think I'm his girlfriend." She shrugged. "And I like him. So I go along with it."

"That's all it is? Going along with him?"

"Sure."

"Does Tom treat you okay?" I said.

She kept her eyes down. "Not always."

"What does he do?"

"He gets mad sometimes."

"Mad how?"

"I mean, he has a temper."

"I've noticed."

"We get in fights. Knockdown fights. He hits me."

"Excuse me?"

"I mean, we hit each other. It's like wrestling."

"How, like wrestling?" I tried to control my thumping heart.

"We have these fights. I don't know—it's weird." She shrugged. "Don't tell him I told you."

I said nothing.

"Eric?" She looked at me. "Okay? Don't say anything to him."

"Okay."

"I'm serious. Don't tell anyone."

Her eyes were pleading and frank, but my mouth had parched with idiot rage. She was waiting for an answer.

Reluctantly, tightly: "Okay."

xxxi

The next day at lunch, I sat with Doug and Doug. My eyes and brain felt so clouded with anger that I couldn't focus on what anybody said. Tom was stretched alone on the grass not far from us, white gaucho hat covering his face, so after a while I wandered over and squatted next to him, crunching Cheez-Its from a plastic bag.

"Hey," I said, and complimented him on the hat.

Tom lifted the brim and glared.

"Where'd you get it, again?"

"Downtown."

"Where, downtown?"

"Some Spanish section."

"The Spaniards moved out of L.A. a long time ago, Tom."

"Well, whatever. Beaner. Pachuco."

"Am I bugging you?"

"Yeah, you really are."

"You trying to take a nap?"

He lifted the hat again and squinted, threateningly.

"How's the coke business?" I said.

He hissed, "I don't talk about that here, okay? Get out of my *space.*"

"Have you paid off Miles yet?"

Now he got to his feet and picked up the backpack he'd been using for a pillow. "You are really irritating." He adjusted his hat and squinted. "Go talk to your little D&D buddies, man, don't bother me."

And he stalked off toward the lunch corral.

The lunch corral got its name from an old sign painted on one of the wooden overhangs enclosing the cafeteria's concrete yard. A profile of our horse mascot, painted around 1962, loomed in the shadows with the words MUSTANG CORRAL written in yellow and green, our school colors. The idea was that we were all Mustangs, frisky and spirited. Tom entered the corral, sat on one of the handrails near the cafeteria window with his gaucho hat, and started bumming change, like the lank junkie at the Olympic. Other kids—I couldn't believe this—but other kids *handed him money*. His hat-shadowed face and fleering eyes intimidated dozens of students, even the ones who saw him every day, and his scam seemed to rest on the loose idea that saying no was uncool—not just uptight, but insulting.

"Low on cash?" I asked him.

"Go away."

"Where's your horse, cowboy?"

"Fuck you."

I neighed at him—*"Nyeeeea-a-a-a!"*

"Shut *up*, will you? Damn."

"Whoa, doggie."

"Dweeb."

xxxii

The following Saturday, Tom and Greta came to our house for lunch. He carried a bag with all the albums Rick had bought us at Hi-Fi. "I don't need 'em anymore," he said. "I don't listen to 'em. They're yours, if you want." And he dropped them with a clatter on the plastic lid of my turntable.

"Sick of them?"

"That Otis Redding shit is like *ancient*," he said.

"But it's not bad."

"It's *old*." He twisted his face in disgust. "Melody's on its way out, anyway. It's old-school."

I laughed. "Where'd you hear that?"

"What do you mean, where'd I hear it? I just *said* it. It came out of my mouth, then I heard it. Fucking-a, Eric, what's your problem?"

What bugged me wasn't Tom's abuse: I was used to that. It was his willingness to reject Rick's albums that felt intimidating. Tom and I both idolized Rick with something more than healthy respect, so any resistance to his ideas was blasphemous.

"Dylan sings like a fucking goat, anyway," Tom said.

"You mean compared to Jello Biafra? At least he can play guitar."

Tom raised his eyebrows, and his face looked amused. I must have blurted this out with more bitterness than I realized, because after a moment he said, "You've been acting weird lately, Eric."

Here we go. "Weird, how?"

"You've been kind of . . . passive-aggressive."

"Whaddayou mean, passive-aggressive?"

"It's like you're pissed at me for something."

"Oh. Well. Maybe I am."

"You mind telling me what it is?"

He sat on the edge of my bed with his elbows on his knees, gazing up with an earnest, open expression. He managed to make *me* feel guilty. How did he do that?

"It's—I just think—you've been obnoxious lately," I said. "Kind of a bully."

"To who?"

"To everyone, Tom. To like most of the school."

"Who says?"

"I do. I've noticed."

"Is it just you?"

"What's that supposed to mean?"

"Who else is saying this?"

"No one. Just me."

"Well, then who made you the fucking judge?"

"Nobody."

"That's right, nobody." Tom got up and started to pace the room. "And I'd rather not deal with any of your fucking opinions, because that's all they really are—they're just *opinions*. They're just your point of view."

"So?"

"So nobody made you God all of a sudden. Right? Your point of view might be wrong. Are you God?"

It sounded like a rhetorical question. I didn't answer, but thought about how every freshman learned to tell fact from opinion with

Mr. Cantwell in the spring. Tom kept glaring at me with his feverish eyes.

"Are you God?"

"No."

"Okay, then. So you don't know everything."

"I know I don't."

And that was as far as we got.

xxxiii

From then on, Tom and I were enemies. I nursed a secret rage and wondered how I could free Rachel from his petty domination. As far as I could tell, I was the only person with even a clue about their strange relationship, and it seemed clear that Rachel would have been a lot better off without him. For the first time in my short life, I felt what you might call a heroic longing. My motives were not quite pure, but I knew there was no one else in the world who could save this beautiful girl from the wrath of her maniac boyfriend.

I dreamed about a peaceful future when Rachel and I could hold hands in public, or eat lunch on the cinder-block wall without some fraudulent cocaine cowboy hanging around. Tom thought he was cool; he pretended to swagger like an outlaw, but the truth was that he bruised and battered the best thing that had ever happened to him, someone I happened to adore. How did you deal with someone so hugely irrational? Why didn't he just *go away?* I tried to think of a strategy to ease Rachel away from Tom's poisonous influence—physically, if I had to, since Rachel still seemed to like him. Tom's insolent stony face and angled gaucho hat filled me with so much rage that when I glanced in the mirror during these weeks in the spring I was always surprised to find a fairly insecure-looking teenager, stoop-shouldered and glum, brooding with dark ambivalent eyes.

The trouble was cowardice. I had plenty of confidence in my own convictions, but no guts to act on them. At sixteen my whole idea of courage was skewed. To me Harold Ivins was brave because he did as he pleased. He was all ego and sinew—insolence backed by a lineman's shoulders. I'd been raised to believe I was better than him for just that reason. I didn't swagger, holler, punch, or insist—I was a nice Jewish boy. I thought unassertiveness amounted to virtuous humility. To me the pecking order of bravery as well as conceited pride in our neighborhood went, in descending order:

Harold

Tom

Eric Sperling

The pleasure I took in my own virtue is sickening to think about now. I was a first-class shlemiel. In English that year, we learned "shlemiel" had more meanings than the everyday one I knew—in class it meant a holy fool, someone who bumbles his way to heaven. With our teacher, Mrs. Printz, we read *Gimpel the Fool*, which seemed like a fairy tale more than anything else, and *Peter Schlemihl*, an old German novel about a man who sold his shadow to the devil. Without his shadow, Schlemihl felt like a freak. When he tried to buy it back, the devil wanted his soul in exchange.

Now I can see the book as an allegory—Schlemihl was a fool because he wanted to be spotless and pure—but in high school it just struck me as a pretty good read. I never thought it might have anything to do with me. And Mrs. Printz, God save her, never tried to clarify anything. She had frizzy black hair tied in a bun, a lumpy body, and narrow heavy glasses that magnified her cloudy pupils to the size of quarters. She found value in any essay we wrote. It was not part of her liberal sensibility to suggest to us how to understand a novel. In fact, I'm not even sure she could read our essays. To manage printed pages, she needed a magnifying glass, so our inky handwriting must have been some kind of torturous, weedy tangle. One rumor went that Robin Lansing had submitted an essay with a two-paragraph introduction, a one-paragraph conclusion, and a four-page exposition that was simply a series of q's. He got a B+.

Anyway, I was so focused on not acting bossy or overbearing that my anger at Tom came out backwards. Instead of confronting him about Rachel, I acted like his friend. Instead of calling him a fraud and a poser, I thought I could learn to judge, disinterestedly, whatever he was up to. I didn't know everything, as he had pointed out. I wasn't God, so I was never likely to know the full story of his relationship with Rachel or, for that matter, the full story of anything else. I wanted to undo myself, vanish, and learn—somehow—the pure unmitigated truth. With this mission in mind, I shared my chips with Tom at lunch. I told him jokes. I helped him out at work. I was like Rick, the scruffy son of privilege, dressing down my rage.

After school we hung out at Mr. B's, listening to music behind the counter the way Rick Fisher had ten years before. Bartholomew disappeared into an office at the back and let us handle customers. For some reason he trusted Tom. Under the old man's watery eye, Tom had learned to price and stock liquor, count in shipments, watch for excess back-stock of beer and soda, and even write a rough order list on the insides of cigarette cartons torn up for scratch paper. He wore pens behind his ear and answered the phone faithfully.

One afternoon, Bartholomew asked him, "Could you check on Gatorade prices over at Thrifty? I think maybe I'll have a sale."

"Which flavors?"

"Just the original green. Red and orange aren't worth bothering about."

Tom nodded and scribbled a note on a cardboard list.

"Anything else?"

"Check their jug wine."

Mr. B started price wars with Thrifty by hanging huge banners in his traffic-facing window: GATORADE HALF OFF. BUD 12-PACKS ONLY $6.99. Before a war, though, he needed certain intelligence, and it was Tom's job to write down the enemy's prices. Sometimes I helped. We were low-level corporate spies.

Tom found his backpack, slung it from one shoulder, and glanced at me.

"You coming?"

"Sure."

We went out. As we wandered across the sun-beaten lot, I watched him scan the strip mall with his narrow eyes. He seemed nervous, as if he expected to meet someone we knew. Inside the store, he said, "Get the Gatorade," and tore off a slab of a cigarette box. "I'll do the wine."

"Okay."

I scribbled some prices, but the fluorescent lights and swooning soft rock in the drink aisle started to irritate me and made the whole project hard to justify. What was I *doing* here? I wondered. I didn't even get paid! *Tom* got paid! How did he use me like this? Suddenly I wanted to throw Tom through the glass doors of the cooler and watch his limp body bring down shelves of soda and fruity drinks. In a blast of anger, I crumpled up the cardboard.

"Hey." Tom had finished pricing the wine and turned up next to me. "You get 'em?"

"Yeah, right here."

"What happened?"

"Oh. Sorry. A little accident."

"Jeez, Eric, can't you even write down a couple of prices? Mr. B can't read it like this."

"So copy it onto yours. No big deal."

"What happened?"

"I got mad at the Gatorade."

Tom shook his head. It only backed up his opinion of me. "Fucking passive-aggressive, man, I swear."

We went out and loitered on the covered sidewalk in front of the store. "Let's wait here," he said. He pulled a pack of cigarettes from his bag and lit one with matches from Mr. B's. "You want one?"

"No thanks."

We watched after-work traffic move in and out of the lot. Sunlight glanced off the cracked pavement, and off the windows of angled cars.

"Did I tell you about Rachel's grandpa?" he said.

"I don't think so."

He raised his eyebrows and blew a stream of smoke. "It's pretty funny. Her relatives are up from Mexico again, for her dad's birthday or something. I went over the other night to meet 'em, and her grandpa asked me what I did for a living. He's this short guy, all wrinkled, kind of rich-looking with a sloppy suit and tie. So I tell him I work in a liquor store. He goes, 'How old are you?' I say fifteen. Her grandpa shrugs, thinks about it, and says, 'If you marry my granddaughter, I buy you a liquor store.'"

"You're kidding."

"No." Tom pulled on his cigarette. "And *he's* not, either. He goes, 'I buy you a liquor store, like my store in Guadalajara.' He owns a silver shop down there or something. 'We have—big wedding.' He says this in English. 'I give you pig to roast. You get married from the priest, we roast a pig, we have firecrackers. ¿Sí? Big wedding. Then I buy you a liquor store, you don't gotta work for no boss, and you give our granddaughter a nice life. Then—grandchildren. *Great*-grandchildren. Okay?' "

"Hah. What'd you say?"

"I didn't know what to say. Finally Rachel's dad says, 'He's working in a liquor store just for right now, Papa. I don't think he wants to do that the rest of his life.' "

"Hmmm. Maybe he does," I suggested.

"Yeah, maybe not," Tom said bitterly.

He threw away his half-smoked cigarette. A fried-fat smell wafted across the lot from Kentucky Fried Chicken. The slanting sun had the tired yellow color of old newspapers. People moved under it without enthusiasm.

"Hey," I said. "Is that Harold?"

"Should be."

"Are you waiting for him?"

"Yup."

Harold came from the direction of Mr. B's. The usual mocking smile was gone and he squinted at me without saying a word. "Sorry I'm late," he said to Tom.

"No big deal."

"It sucks we can't do this at school."

"The narcs'll see us."

"Fucking Larry." Harold said. "Well, let's go somewhere private." He glanced at me. "You coming?"

"I guess so."

Tom led us around to a puddled alley in back of the store. He unslung his backpack. I watched him trade a brown bag with coke in it for a wad of Harold's money. "This is the same stuff as before?" Harold asked.

"Same stuff, yeah. Same guy. Cándido Flambón."

Harold lit a cigarette and said to me, "I was wrong about your friend here. He's well-connected. I wouldn't believe it if the coke wasn't so pure, but your friend's hooked *up.*"

He smiled, and Tom looked proud. His cocaine-cowboy image was backed with honest goods. Maybe impressing Harold was actually the point: I wondered if Tom's shtick at school was just an answer to the way Ryker and the others had treated him. If so, it had worked. His new image was a success. He was a badass, a local outlaw, and why should he want to be anything else as long as Harold Ivins, of all people, mantled him with an aura of smugglers and distant gunfire?

xxxiv

A week later, on a drizzling afternoon, Rachel and I were stretched on my bed after school, watching the sky outside grow a dismal shade of grey. My bedroom window looked out on the front yard. Palm trees drooped and the air smelled like rain-freshened street. I felt quiet, alert. I decided to ask Rachel a question that was lingering at the back of my mind.

"How long have you known Maui?" I said.

"I don't know, about a year. Why?"

"He's interesting."

"Yeah, he's lived all over. Maui's been through a lot already."

"What do you mean?"

"Well, he and his mom moved away from Jamaica when he was a kid. I think they lived with some relatives in Hawaii. He went to college there, but didn't graduate because he fell in love with some Hawaiian girl he still talks about, and followed her to L.A. Something like that. He used to be a real romantic."

"He's not now?"

"Huh." Rachel smiled. "Not Maui."

I kept quiet, hoping she would explain. She didn't.

"Are you having an affair with him?"

Without looking over, she nodded.

"You are?"

"Do I sleep with him sometimes? Sure."

"Tom doesn't know that?"

"Of course not. He doesn't know about you, either."

She pulled her legs to her chest and locked her arms around them playfully.

"How are things with Tom, anyway?"

"Not too bad, I guess."

"Any fights?"

She was quiet.

"I noticed you don't have as many bruises."

"We haven't been hanging out as much. Outside school."

"What do you fight about, anyway?"

"We just get mad and fight. Like brother and sister."

"Oh."

"He starts it or whatever, but it's not like I don't hit back. We *wrestle.*" She smiled emptily. "That's what happened with Jeremy."

"What do you mean?"

"They got into a wrestling match after school one day at Granger. Tom grabbed Jeremy's dick, and everyone saw. That's why they used to call him a faggot."

"He told me he grabbed Jeremy's ass."

Rachel chuckled. "That was afterwards. That just made things worse. But Tom says Jeremy had a hard-on when he grabbed him. Which is really funny, when you think about it—those two fighting like little puppies."

I tried to absorb this information.

"Anyway, for me it's getting kind of old. Even when we don't fight, he gets on my nerves." She held her knees, musing, and shrugged. "He expects a lot. He can be kind of a baby. And I think he's getting hooked on cocaine."

"I haven't noticed that."

"Well, if he's not addicted, he's at least selling it more than he should. It must be like a month since he paid off Miles."

"Are you sure?"

"I'm just guessing."

Talking to Rachel was instructive.

"You said Maui's not romantic," I said, "but he seems like a pretty big ladies' man."

"Oh, he's a big *ladies'* man. He's just not romantic about it." She smiled, then released her legs. "After that one Hawaiian girl, he hasn't gone with anyone as just, like, their boyfriend. I think it really changed him. He didn't always look like he does—he was really straight before. I've seen pictures. He had short hair and worked in a hospital, with his mom, who's a nurse. He wore these hospital-orderly clothes. And his real name's not Maui. He just started calling himself that when he went into the pot business."

"What's his real name?"

Rachel gave a short laugh. "Leonard Ford."

"Really?" I said. "Leonard?"

"Leonard *Ford*," she repeated.

We listened to the rain fall, dripping from the telephone wire and soaking the grass. I felt happy in spite of the weather. By now I was deeply in love with Rachel: Her dark eyes, the trust in her voice, and the easy, womanly way she treated me in bed all worked a deep and heartsickening influence. If I'd been less concerned about my masculinity, I would have drawn flowers on my notebooks at school. Our afternoons were getting wilder and more indulgent every week; we did acrobatic things that grew from a startling animal hunger. But it was horrible afterwards, because the hang-ups that evaporated in bed came thundering back when I was alone, and even if I shrugged off the usual objections to sleeping with somebody's girl-friend, I still had enough personal conscience to hate the wheedling lies I had to tell. This was how denial happened! Maybe it was the secret of our town! Could it be true? Hordes of bright-eyed, tie-wearing, casually dressed, outwardly cheerful people, walking around with their heads full of lies about sex? This was how you became one of *them!* Oh, sweet Jesus, what a punishment!

Rachel's backpack lay on the floor beside the bed, and spilling out of it was a handful of plastic-wrapped pieces of skull-shaped sugar candy.

"What are these?" I reached over to look at one.

She chuckled. "Don't you know? Those are *calaveras.* Day of the Dead candy."

"You celebrate Day of the Dead?"

"We don't, but my aunts bring us candy from Mexico."

"Are they any good?"

"They're just sugar."

I studied the little skull. Except for two depressions at the eyes and cheeks, most of the detail was painted brightly onto the pinkish crystallized paste. "I guess I've never thought about the name of our town before," I said.

"It's from a graveyard the Spanish found," she said.

"Really?"

"I think so. Like some Indian graveyard, by the water. The Spaniards found all these bones and named the beach after that."

"Hm."

Rachel yawned. It was about four in the afternoon. The sound of tires stroking the pavement came lazily through the window.

"Is that Tom's car?" Rachel said.

"What?"

I flipped onto my stomach. The blue Chrysler was out there. Its underside scraped as it eased into the driveway, where it would be obscured from the street. "Shit." I jumped up and started putting on clothes. "I'll try to get rid of him."

Rachel pulled the covers over her head. "Pretend you just got up from a nap," she suggested. "You look all sleepy."

Tom honked, and when I didn't come out, he stomped onto the deck and knocked on the clattering French doors. I answered with a bleary expression. He was out of breath.

"Come on," he said. "I need your help."

"What for?"

"Just come on."

"Can you slow down a minute? You woke me up."

"What, is it nap time?" His face broke into a grin. He had on a sweatshirt, a rolled knit cap, and the combat boots from Halloween. He pushed past me, into the door. "At least gimme a glass of water."

"Wait—"

"Come *on*, Eric, I'm in a goddamn hurry!" He wheeled around. "Put your shoes on and let's *go*."

"How come you're in a hurry?"

"I'll tell you in the car."

He stalked to the kitchen for water.

Since I'd answered the door without shoes, I shuffled back to my room, where a Rachel-shaped lump on the bed was lying very still.

"I'm just putting on sneakers," I whispered, "and then I'm leaving."

"Where you going?" asked the lump.

"Don't know yet. Just be gone when I get back."

The dead-end front hallway outside my bedroom connected to the dining room where the French doors were. With my shoes on, I darted into the hallway and almost rammed into Tom, who stood calmly in the dining room with a glass of water. He still wore that obnoxious grin. Had he heard anything?

"Ready?"

I nodded.

The car's interior smelled like cigarettes, and when we pulled into the street, Tom reached up for a pack of Marlboros clamped in the visor. He lit one from the dash lighter, filled the car for a second with the smell of toasted tobacco, then blew smoke out the window and drove hunched over, stealthily, as if he wanted to hide. He turned up a Dead Kennedys tape.

"Why don't you tell me what we're doing?" I said.

"I need your help getting that fish off the wall."

"The marlin?"

"Yeah."

"Why's it coming off the wall?"

"It's a chore. My mom asked me to do it."

"What does your mom want it off the wall for?"

"To clean it."

"You mean, dust it? You need help dusting it?"

"We have to bring it to a cleaner's," he said in a choked-off voice. "Now shut up about it. The thing's heavy. My mom asked me to get it down, I can't get it down by myself. Okay? That's all."

I had no experience with stuffed fish. For all I knew, Tom was telling the truth. He kept driving with the same hunched-over posture and flicked his cigarette out the window. Soon we pulled up to the front of Windsor Gardens. The gate there consisted of two fancy, wrought-iron grilles hinged to a pair of phony rock columns. A number pad was perched on a curving pole beside the car window. Tom found a pair of gloves under his seat and put one on before tapping in a code. The gate swung open. He saw me staring.

"Fingerprints," he explained.

We steered through the damp tar streets and pulled into the Lindens' cul-de-sac, where, even in the rain, a statue of Cupid spat water. Their garage gaped open. Tom backed the Chrysler in and told me, "My mom's got the remote. I had to leave it open like this. That's why I was in such a hurry."

We got out, and he touched a button on the wall behind the water heater. The garage door tilted and jangled closed. Now the Chrysler was hidden. He flicked on a fluorescent light over Mr. Linden's old workbench that filled the garage with a buzzing white glare.

"Take some gloves out of the car," he ordered. "Under your seat."

"Why do I need a pair?"

"Just do it."

"You are really acting weird."

The inside of the condo was white and cool, as usual, but somehow draftier. The marlin arched over the fireplace with a startled expression. Tom had set a chair in front of it. Now he got another chair, and I helped him lift the marlin carefully off of three notched metal bolts buried in the plaster. There were seams in the silver skin where the head and tail had been cut. Mr. Linden had told me once that the middle was fake. They'd eaten the meat, and a taxidermist had replaced it with a painted block of wood.

I said, "It doesn't seem that dirty. We could probably just dust it off."

"Shut *up*, will you? Damn."

I helped him carry the fish to the garage. Tilting the marlin into the backseat of the Chrysler was awkward because of the way it curved out from its wooden mount. "Does your mom even know you have a car?" I said. "How did she expect you to do this when you don't have a car?"

"I promised I'd do it."

"You're not gonna tell me anything, are you?"

His mouth made a tight seam.

I said, "Alright, well, I have to pee."

I was halfway across the living room toward the bathroom door when Tom said, "No! Fuck," but I flicked on the light before he could reach me. A damp breeze pulled through the window. The delicate sheer curtains had been torn and the screen lay bent on the carpet. Tom was grabbing my shoulder.

"What happened here?" I said.

"Nothing happened."

"Will you just tell me? Did you break the screen?"

"Someone did."

"Yeah, no kidding." I wrenched away from him. "Are you trying to make it look like someone broke in? Why?"

He shifted on his feet. "Can we go?"

"What's going on?"

"Don't try and get moral with me."

"I'm just asking a question."

"Don't try and fucking judge me."

"Tom."

He looked down at his boots, red-faced. At last he said, "Miles keeps hounding me for money."

"So you're stealing the fish?"

Tom was quiet.

"And making it look like someone else broke in? How much could that thing be worth?"

"I saw one in a pawnshop for five hundred bucks."

"Where?"

"In Inglewood."

This was hard to believe, but, like I said, I knew nothing about stuffed fish.

"So, your mom's supposed to think someone broke in here just to get that marlin?"

"No, I went through one of her drawers in the bedroom and took stuff she'll get insurance for. Look." He took me to the green-toned room. One drawer from the bureau lay spilled on the flowery bed, but otherwise the room was clean.

I nodded. "Selective thief."

"You think it looks fake?"

"Not *fake*. It just looks . . . suspicious."

"What do you mean?"

"Well, how come no one touched the stereo? or the TV?"

"They just wanted small things."

"Like the fish?"

Tom narrowed his eyes. His soft face was thoughtful. Finally he smiled. "I'll take something from my room, too. That'll work."

He went to his room at the end of the hall and came out with the Atari game. Joysticks swung down from thin wires. He carried it to the garage and tossed it into the car. When he came back, I lost my temper. "This is your *house*, Tom," I hollered. "You're stealing from your own mom!"

"What do you care?"

"She's our friend!"

"She's not really my mom."

His face went cold, staring straight into the room. Now I was supposed to feel sympathy.

"Look, I'm sorry," I said. "I know you think your mom can afford it, and I know you're being an anarchistic badass or whatever, but did it ever occur to you that maybe you're also being a jerk?"

His eyes darted at me. "Have you ever had a drug dealer riding your ass for money?" For some reason, he waited for an answer. "I didn't think so. You have no idea how it feels," he said.

"Well, how come you owe so much money? Haven't you paid off Miles?"

"I did, but I'm in debt again."

"How come?"

His features hardened. He didn't answer. At first I felt scared, but I was also tired of backing down, sick of feeling like Tom's little partner in everything we did. So I said, "I'll tell my parents about this."

Quick as a snake, he grabbed my collar and squeezed my neck, hard, with both wrists, jerked my face toward him, and stared sullenly into it, with so much strength in his hands that the urge to cross him slumped at the bottom of my chest.

"You fucking do that and I'll kill you," he hissed. He was tense, trembling. "Okay?"

"Okay."

"And don't tell Rachel, either."

I nodded.

"I don't want anyone to know."

My nerves were lit with adrenaline and spots of color danced in my eyes. Then it was over. Tom let go and stalked back to the garage. He pushed the button to open the clanking door and I went around to the passenger side. For a few tense seconds the Chrysler idled in public view, and I sat half-ducked under the marlin's nose, looking at the statue of Cupid while Tom ran back to the garage. With no remote, he had to push the button again and run out, ducking under the door as it lowered, jump into the car, and wheel it around. He chirped the tires and left a mark on the pavement by mistake.

We parked on a street just outside Windsor Gardens, where Tom usually hid the Chrysler. He would drive the fish to a pawnshop later. We pulled the green canvas hood over the car and walked back to my house through the dismal, damp-smelling streets. I was nervous about Rachel until we got home, but of course she wasn't there. Tom and I pretended to do homework at my house for about two hours, and he left a fake message on his mom's machine saying we'd gone there straight from school.

part five

XXXV

The Zohar describes evil as a disturbance in nature, intrinsic to it but not exactly "natural"—more of a blindness or resistance to vibrations from above. The idea is that it's a passive force, which as far as I can tell doesn't mean quiet, or mute. Just the opposite: Evil can be noisy, bustling, busy, pompous, ignorant, clumsy, or pretentious, as well as malevolent or cruel. Evil doesn't listen. That's the main idea. It never pays attention. It's the *opposite* of attention. For monks and holy people in every tradition, a meditative silence is the highest kind of reverence to God, and there's even a myth I found somewhere about a catapult, used by a pair of angels, for the purpose of flinging an impure *nefesh* back and forth until all the world's dirt falls away and it can hear the higher or finer vibrations. I am not making this up. I haven't experienced it myself, but apparently the angels stand on opposite ends of the world and hurl the stubborn soul through the heavens in this tremendous *kaf ha-kelah*, or catapult, to make it quiet down.

• • •

Our train pulls out of the railyard. Rodney sits just high enough on the barley now to look over the rim as the wheels start to clack. "Come on, pick it up," he growls. "We've been here long enough." After the delay in Bakersfield, we moved on to some smaller town in the Central Valley. The sun here is intense. Yardworkers have been lazy as dogs about getting the train to move, and the iron machinery itself feels bloated, sluggish—as if a central California summer could turn even solid rolling stock molten and soft. The train clatters along with the same lumbering deliberation even after we clear the yard.

Arid fields of cotton stretch for miles on either side of the train, studded here and there with oil rigs, iron hobbyhorses, rocking under the summer heat.

• • •

Rachel turned out to be right: Calaveras Beach was named for an ancient Indian burial ground. The missionaries must have meant it as a warning, a sort of label of desolation. They'd named the village north of ours after Santa Monica, Los Angeles belonged to Our Lady Queen of Angels, and so on; but *la playa de las calaveras* took its profane name from the human skeletons that were its outstanding physical feature, yellowed remains lying half-revealed in dunes and weeds near the waterline.

I read about this in an encyclopedia when I was still in school. Priests had named the local Calaveras-area tribe "Gabrielino," after the mission at San Gabriel where they were baptized. I read about the mission period, and the disastrous program of self-improvement the Spaniards built onto the lives of people who had managed well enough for thousands of years. On the same land where a Gabrielino man could, once upon a time, wake up late and spend a lazy afternoon collecting acorns, fish, army worms, rabbits, or anything his wife might cook into a stew, there was suddenly a monkish system of adobe buildings and Latin chants, whip-discipline, foreign disease, and rows of beans and barley that needed planting and picking, all for the sake of monks who weren't used to field work.

The effect this information had on me as a teenager was electrifying. The news that the country you've been raised in is not the same as the mythic nation you've been taught to love can be nearly as confusing, to a kid, as the bad news that caused Oedipus to claw out his eyes. I had *not* worked all my life to get good grades only to be blindsided by some sort of rottenness at the core of my country and town. No! It was unacceptable. The rest of the nation might be guilty, implicated, bloodstained, but not me. I felt vengeful on *behalf* of the Indians. It seemed like my duty. Ever since the night by the bonfire with Rick my politics had shifted enough to make me insurgent, incendiary, meaning, for the most part, a pain in the ass to my parents. Rather than humbling me, the things I learned gave me an excuse to be insolent, and I started to dissociate myself completely from Calaveras Beach, like a disillusioned passenger trying to excuse himself from the Titanic.

xxxvi

"Go ahead!" my dad snapped one night at dinner, after I made some smart remark about the bourgeoisie. He threw down his fork and argued back with his thrust-forward face—eyes insulted, mustache bristling. "Tell me what happened, if you know so much about it. Explain to me about Hitler."

"Well, he exploited the middle class. Their complacency. They went along with him."

"*Who* went along with him? Be specific."

"The burghers. The professional townspeople. The yuppies back then."

My dad touched a napkin to his lips. He finished chewing and arranged the napkin neatly next to his plate, eyes lowered, patient with me to a fault. "Just for your information, Eric," he said at last, in a calm voice, "Hitler attacked the 'yuppies back then.' On his way up, he bashed the bourgeoisie, which was partly Jewish."

I shook my head. "That's not true! The Jews were mostly artists and Communists! That's why Hitler hated them. They were outsiders, just like Indians were after white people came here."

"Well, that's the cliché," my dad admitted. "But Jews were also bankers and financiers, professors and journalists. They were very well integrated. It's wrong to think Hitler was anti-Semitic just because Jews were all left-wing, or somehow lower-class. In fact, his friend Goebbels was a Communist. The Nazis came to power because the German economy was in the toilet—which meant that Hitler could act like the mean old money-grubbing Jews were oppressing *him*." Dad's eyes were dark but emotional. "It was about class feeling, you're absolutely right. But it was feeling against the rich. At least at first. You understand? Class feeling gave them a reason to kill."

"Well, I just mean the conformism—"

"Conformism happens on every level, Eric, not just in the middle class."

"Walter."

My mom stared bitterly. World War II was not her favorite subject. She also hated this father-son strain at the table. When we had both taken in her wounded expression, she glanced away, and for a while there was only the sound of clanking silverware and a distant stream of news from the radio upstairs.

After a while, my mom said, "Greta still hasn't heard about the robbery."

"Oh, no?" Dad stirred the food on his plate. "Well, I guess it may not be worth the officers' time."

"I suppose not."

"Did they find fingerprints?" I asked.

"No, but Greta says there was a tire mark on the driveway, by the garage. It looks as if the burglars climbed in and out through the bathroom. And Greta had her car at work. Nobody can make sense of it." She shook her head and frowned. "Of course, Greta could have made the tire mark herself."

"She doesn't remember doing it?" my dad said.

My mother shrugged. "She says no."

Then silence at the table again, thickened by heat from the kitchen. It took a huge amount of willpower to sit there without giving myself away. I almost said, "Tom and I did it." The words came out clearly in my imagination, and I could visualize the results. But I ran up against an absolute lack of will to watch my parents turn their unbelieving faces in my direction and ask me what I was talking about.

"Well, at least it could have been worse," said my dad.

"I suppose," said my mom.

For a few seconds I tried to fend off guilt by holding up, like a shield, the idea that my parents and Greta were silly middle-class adults with an overdeveloped sense of propriety. But the air had gone out of that argument. It seemed entirely beside the point. My mom's mouselike face looked wrinkled, almost old. Her German accent grew melancholically thin, and I could tell that to her this felt like a waking nightmare, as if some tentacle of the barbarous, drug-addled population of downtown L.A. had finally penetrated our circle of friends.

xxxvii

One day in April, I biked with Rachel to Maui's after school with the idea of going surfing, and we found him sorting and deseeding an enormous load of marijuana on the coffee table. He ate from a bowl of bread pudding that gave off a warm peach-apple smell.

"You can't cook, can you?" said Rachel. "Where'd you get this?"

"My mother, she got a big vat of it in ha' fridge."

"Where's your mom live again?"

"Gardena."

"You don't see her much, do you?"

"Every mont', I take the bus."

"Oh."

Maui nodded, and went back to work.

"Does she know you do this for a living?" Rachel asked.

"Yeah she does." Maui smiled. "She's a Jamaica woman, she t'inks it should be legalized. To her, I'm just a businessman."

"Your mom's Jamaican?" I asked.

He turned his eyes on me. Rachel had given me some idea of Maui's past, but I wanted the story from him. This was the first time I'd ever heard him speak English for any length of time. His Caribbean accent emphasized end-syllables: Legal*ized*, he said. Garden*a*.

"I mean—you're from Hawaii, your mom's from Jamaica, but you both live here now?"

"Yeah." He smiled. "I been all over the world." He covered the pot with a sheet of tinfoil and sat on the edge of the couch. His legs were spread wide and his elbows rested on his knees, with his fingers laced in the middle. "Great long heartbreak story."

I wanted to hear it, but someone knocked on the door. Maui opened it and we saw Tom and Robin Lansing, the class president, standing outside. Tom wore his backpack from school. Maui let them in and offered around the bread pudding, then sat again at his coffee table.

A silence came over the room. Robin said, "Tom wants to ask you something."

Maui nodded toward him. "What's up?"

From his green canvas backpack Tom drew a brick of coke and placed it on the table. "I wanted to ask you about selling this," he said. "It's kind of a lot, and I was gonna sell half of it to Robin. But he can't afford all of it. I heard you deal coke sometimes."

"Some*times.*"

"I thought we could have like a tasting, and if it's good stuff, you could take it off my hands right now."

"How much you sellin' it for?"

Tom named a price that seemed outrageously high to me.

"Cheap," said Maui. "That's rock-bottom."

"You want to try some?"

He was still leaning forward with his elbows on his knees, and he paused for a moment before standing. "I stay away from cocaine, you know? I don't like to get caught wit' it." But he rooted in a cabinet under his TV for a mirror, a razor-blade, and a tiny brass pipe. He sat and arranged six skinny lines on the mirror, sniffed one for himself, and passed it around the table. The mirror seemed to trail a wave of sinus trouble; everyone made snorting sounds.

"Pure," said Maui. "Where'd it come from?"

"Some friend of Rick Fisher's."

"He said he got it from a Colombian," said Robin.

"Nicaraguan," Tom corrected. "The coke's Colombian."

"Oh."

Now Maui was staring hard at Tom, brown eyes veined and serious.

"What Nicaraguan?" he said. "Flambón?"

"Yeah, that's his name."

"You met him?"

"No. This guy Miles told me."

"I don't do no business with fucking Cándido Flambón."

Maui started to clear the coffee table of all the coke paraphernalia.

"Why? Who is he?"

"Cándido Flambón is right-wing," Maui said. "You know what *contra* means?"

We all shook our heads.

"You don't know not'ing about politics. You know Michael Manley, in Jamaica?"

We shook our heads again.

"Okay, let me 'splain it to you, one step at a time. And after dat you got to promise me not to go back to Flambón. Okay?" He looked at us all very seriously. "Now, see—I spend most a my life in Jamaica. Not Hawaii. This Maui name, is just somet'ing I got from a girlfriend. In Hawaii, Samoa, New Zealand, you know, he a big hero—Maui pull islands from the sea, bring fire to the people. I use it like a cover-up. It don't mean not'ing. People buy my stuff an' t'ink they smoking Maui-Wowie, finest Hawaiian shit. Right? It don't mean not'ing. All a dis"—he gestured toward the tinfoil— "come from Jamaica.

"My family live in Jamaica when Manley got kicked out. Michael Manley, big socialist president an' all a dat. My family, too, you know, we don't like none a' dese right-wing shits put up in Kingston by the United States. So we emigrate after Manley got kicked out and we set up in Miami. We got friends in Jamaica need help, you know, friends of Manley. Dey send us some weed. It sell good in Miami. We send all a' dat money back to Jamaica. It's like a racket, see? But it works. An' you got gangs of Jamaicans all over Miami doin' the same shit for their political friends.

"So my family sell for a while in Miami, but den I get busted an' I don' want to do it no more. Soon my mother and father have a separation, an' my mother move here to L.A. Three years ago. I come, too, and I meet some cute Hawaiian girl. Right? Sexy, sexy. I fall in love. But dat ended. Great long heartbreak story. So I start doin' dis again, sellin' for friends in Miami. We got a pipeline for Jamaican shit goin' all across the country. So I, for the last two years, I raise money for Manley again.

"But Cándido Flambón, you see, he doin' the same damn t'ing, only he come from Nicaragua. In Nicaragua you got Somoza kicked out in 1979, corrupt right-wing Somocista bastards overt'rown by socialists, Sandinistas. Flambón, he got Somocista kinda guys fightin' dem Sandinistas called the *contra*. *La contra-revolución*. I don' like *la contra*, you know? Dey an' I stand for different t'ings. It's like a hot little Cold War in the Caribbean, *Yanquis* and commies, and none a' you goddamn undereducated American kids know a t'ing about it. When you sell cocaine for Flambón, you send money to the worst, the most corrupt soldiers in Central America."

We stared at him, a little bewildered.

"You hear me?"

We nodded.

"So dat's why I ain't gonna help you."

Tom held the mirror in his lap, with the line of coke that I hadn't sniffed. He took up the brass pipe and snorted, half-closing his eyes. Then he made a pig noise deep in his sinuses and rubbed his nose.

"How come you get involved with Flambón, anyway?" Maui asked.

"I owe one of his dealers money."

Maui nodded, his veined eyes full of warring emotion.

"You got to be careful wit' him," he said lightly. "You got to be real careful."

Tom stared at the open package of coke on the table and absorbed what Maui had told us. The couch, the thin carpet, even the walls of the house were thick with the ashen, almost greasy smell of old marijuana. I remember thinking Tom's cocaine-cowboy role had street cred now—that romantic aura of drug smugglers and distant gunfire was no longer quite so faint.

Later in the afternoon the sun burned low on the horizon, reflecting off the water in quivering reddish flares. Rachel sat up straight on her board, spine curved, hands on her legs. She held up one hand to look against the sun for waves, then wiped back her hair and spat salt water from her lips. The mass of slicked hair gave her face the look of an otter or a dog, with large, sad, sensitive eyes.

"How did Tom seem to you?" she asked.

"It was weird he didn't say anything. He barely noticed we were there."

"He might be jealous."

"Of me?"

"Sure. What were we doing at Maui's together?"

"We go to Maui's a lot."

"*He* doesn't know that."

A small set of waves took us by surprise, rolling out of the sun's glare and joggling our boards. I paddled forward to keep my balance.

"He hit me again," she said.

"You're kidding. When?"

"On Monday. He said I was acting cold."

"Where were you?"

"It was after school, on the way to my house. He got pissed at something I said, and kind of knuckled me in the ribs."

"What did you say?"

"I don't know, something sarcastic. But I slapped him back. I said he couldn't do that to me anymore, and he just stared. Then I went home."

"That was it?"

"Pretty much." Rachel squinted at me. "But it was the first time in a while. It kind of surprised me."

A slight current was pulling us both beyond the surf line. I adjusted myself with a back-paddle. My heart had started to pound. I could almost feel the tiny streams of adrenaline squeezing into my blood, and my head raced with wild plans to save Rachel. We could elope, I thought. We could drive the Chrysler to Mexico. We could live like fugitives in a hard, elemental country, far from the misunderstandings of our parents and her seething crazy-eyed boyfriend.

"Why didn't you break up with him right there?"

She shrugged.

"Rachel, he's not going to just stop," I said hotly. "We have to do something."

Her animal eyes turned on me with a flat, frank, low-burning expectation. Sometimes her signals were so mixed that I felt my brain scramble. "Not *we*," she said. "It's my problem, okay? All you have to do is stay out of it."

I spat in the water and looked into the lowering sun. I was all nerves and impotent rage.

"Tom's been under a lot of pressure," she added.

"How come?"

"Harold and those guys keep stealing his coke."

"Stealing it?"

"Well, they took a bunch of it after that day in the bathroom. Now he sells it to them at a cut rate. So he owes more money to Miles."

"That's hard to believe."

Rachel shrugged and squinted at the water. "I don't think he realizes what he's gotten himself into."

Tom's cockiness got worse in the weeks after Maui's little history lesson. The idea that he was two steps away from a shadowy international player like Cándido Flambón had flattered his self-esteem. He thought drug culture was a lush underworld of gangsters and overlords who built shadow empires far from the phoniness of Calaveras High. He figured he was learning to be streetwise while the rest of us worried about grades. He ran his coke business from his bedroom, which looked like a war zone. What had started as a boy's sunshot cube of plaster wall and unmade bed was now a cynical and squalid suburban hole, with Atari cartridges and other useless junk from his closets dragged out and neglected, apparently for no better reason than to hide bits of drug paraphernalia from his mom. Mrs. Linden knew nothing about cocaine, so Tom could afford to be negligent about razor blades and dusty dollar bills, as long as his room was a mess.

I still saw him every weekend, at his house instead of mine, because our mothers had decided to move their weekend lunch to the Lindens'. These Saturdays were boring. Tom would fix his skateboard, or dismantle his telephone, or count his drug money, while I sat on his bed and tried to concentrate on my homework. The lack of anything to do at Windsor Gardens sometimes drove him to snort coke. One Saturday, with both of our mothers in the house, he took out a mirror and snuffed up a line of powder.

"You want some?" he said.

"No, thanks."

"Why not? Let's get high together."

"Nah."

I was sitting on his bed, flipping through a comic book.

"You're scared of your mom," he said.

"No."

"Then come on."

I looked up. What bugged me more than anything having to do with the coke was this personal tension between us. He had guts, I didn't—it was the usual equation, only notched up into a black-market romance of money and drugs.

"No," I said.

He let out a sigh, then picked up his skateboard and tested one of the axles.

"I think Rachel's seeing someone," he said.

"Oh yeah?" I cleared my throat. "How come?"

"I don't know. Two or three weeks ago, it was like she quit being interested in me. Like over the weekend or something. Friday everything was cool, but on Monday she just didn't seem *there* anymore. It's been like that ever since. I don't know what to think."

"Would it surprise you if she was seeing someone else?"

"Surprise me? Sure. She's my girlfriend."

I shrugged. "I don't know, I mean, she's only sixteen."

"So what?"

"So maybe she doesn't like to be tied down."

"What are you saying?"

I shook my head. "I'm not saying anything. I'm just throwing stuff out."

"Do you know anything?"

"Of course not."

"Well, she's been acting weird. That's all I know."

I scratched my arm.

"You have any idea who it could be?" I said.

"No fucking clue. Do you?"

"No."

" 'Cause if you do, I'd like to know about it."

"I'll let you know," I said.

Now my heart pounded as if I'd sucked up six lines of cocaine.

"Oh—" he said, changing the subject. His lightly coked brain skittered like a top. "Did you see this?" He picked up a flyer that read, "TATTOO CONVENTION, TWO DAYS ONLY! MAY 19-20," with a map.

"What is it?"

"It's a thing Rick invited me to. A bunch of tattoo artists get together and show off their work. He said it's like a carnival. I was thinking of going."

"It's today and tomorrow?"

"Yeah," he said absently. Then: "Did you hear about Maui?"

"No."

"He got busted. The police invaded his house."

"You're kidding. When?"

"Yesterday. One of his neighbors called the police, and the cops decided to make an example out of him."

"Jesus."

"It's in the paper today."

He rummaged on his floor for a copy of the *Bulletin*. The headline read LOCAL POT LORD JAILED, and a photograph showed Maui in handcuffs in front of his house, about to be shoved into a squad car by a bunch of cops. He wore a faded T-shirt and stood erect and proud with his eyes aimed straight at the camera. The story used his real name, Leonard Ford, and I tried to imagine what he'd looked like as a crop-haired hospital orderly, straitlaced and quiet, in the days when he'd loved some elusive girl.

"So you wanna go to this thing?" He waved the flyer.

"Now? Really?" I shrugged. "You have the car?"

"It's around the corner."

Why not? "Sure."

The answer seemed to energize him. Tom found his hat in the closet and put on an oversized collared shirt. The shirt had been his dad's—beige and cotton, with a blue band of tropical leaves printed across the middle. He buttoned it over a muscle T-shirt, which he didn't have the muscles for, and the loose baggy sleeves covering his scrawny arms, along with his heavy boots, made him look irritatingly cool. We went out to the living room where our mothers sat with their wine, watching tennis.

"We're going out," Tom said.

"Are you going to the mall?" his mom asked.

"Yup. Play some video games."

"You have enough money?" she asked. My mother smiled. Her face was a little pink.

"From my allowance," Tom said, and we left.

We uncovered the car and drove off. The day was glaring and hot. Beside the smog-stained highway, the trees had been dulled with a layer of dust. Traffic was light, even for a Saturday. We followed the flyer's map to a grim L.A. neighborhood on the edge of Koreatown, where boxlike buildings cluttered each side of the street like random piles of bricks. Signs advertised inventories of chicken meat, or sound equipment, or auto glass, in both English and Korean. Tom squinted at everything and steered the car.

"I think this is it." He parked in a broken-asphalt lot behind a warped chain-link fence, across the street from a church.

"Where?"

"Right there. Rick said it was in a church."

A sign on the sidewalk that must have once shown a name and denomination in mounted plastic letters now read, behind cracked glass, "CORINTH CLUB." Wide steps and a row of heavy columns faced the street. The walls were a pale mossy green, and in the shadows beyond the columns I saw mesh stretched over the doorway, apparently to keep chunks of plaster from falling on people's heads.

"Old church," I said.

"It's a nightclub now."

We went in. A teenage girl took admission money. The main hall, up a flight of stairs, was thick with sweat and smoke and noise, distorted music and the sound of buzzing tattoo guns. Workshop-booths from local parlors were set up behind folding tables, and every workshop had a bright lamp glaring on somebody's arm or belly. Powder blue walls lifted over the mass of people milling, browsing, drinking. Thick smoke curled in front of soft white lamps mounted over wall panels showing the Christian stations of the cross. It was a weird mixture of carnival, club, and shrine. The total effect suggested a voluptuous torture chamber. In one booth, a dark-haired woman leaned over a chair with her lower back exposed to a lamp, holding a beer, eyes closed, dreaming in pain while a bald man etched below her ribs.

"Wow," said Tom.

We pushed through the crowd. Behind a folding table against the right wall we found Rick talking to a muscled bald man who had a bluish spiderweb tattooed across his jaw. Rachel was there, too. Customers flipped through books of designs on the table.

Rick said, "Hey, I didn't know you guys were gonna show up."

"We just decided to. Hi, Rachel," Tom said.

"Hey." She gave him a lukewarm smile.

Rick made a round of introductions. The spiderwebbed man was Amos. While he talked to Rachel in a loud, chatty voice I started to wonder why anybody would ink a permanent design on his face. My sense of irony lit up: Suppose you got sick of it? You'd have to wear a bag. Amos did say that when he wanted to hide the spiderweb, he just grew a beard—"but that means I have to plan my job interviews and visits to the grandparents, like, three weeks in advance." He laughed. I scowled. I didn't like him.

I turned and looked at the teeming crowd. Distorted music and grey smoke swirled together with smells of sweat and patchouli oil. There were bald punks with tattooed heads, bikers with chains on their faces, shirtless gang members showing off mural-sized tattoos between their shoulders, and a woman with bells pierced into the skin of her upper arm. It was another mob of individualists, like the crowd at the Olympic. Many of the tattoos were beautiful—shaded, colorful seascapes, dragons the size of my arm, portraits of Marilyn Monroe or detailed, agonized Christs—and the piercings gave off a primitive tribal threat. But now I had enough distance not to be intimidated. Most of these people, I thought (proudly, scornfully), were acting out their individualism with full force on their *bodies*.

Next to Rick's table, at a piercing booth, there was a beautiful girl maybe seventeen years old, with pale freckled skin and long reddish hair. She nodded and chatted with the piercing matron, and then—unexpectedly—lifted off her shirt.

Amos interrupted, "You gonna get a tattoo?" he asked me.

I shook my head. "Don't they hurt?"

"Just over nerves and bone." He rubbed his jaw. "This one hurt all my hair follicles."

"I bet."

I turned back to the red-haired woman. The piercing lady smoked a cigarette and cleaned a stud gun with a rag. At last she brought out a tray of instruments and turned the girl sideways, under a white-hot lamp. With a clean rag she disinfected the girl's breast and then found a long skewer, like a knitting needle. Now my angle was wrong; all I could see was red hair flowing off a pair of pretty shoulders. But when the piercing lady positioned the needle, I winced. Slim muscles stood out on the girl's freckled back.

"Now, *that* hurts," said Amos.

"I bet."

From out of the crush of people Miles appeared, looking nervous and pale. He gave Tom a nod, without taking off his sunglasses, and started talking to Rick. I watched him pull a cigarette from the brass case in his breast pocket and light up with trembling fingers. He threaded his way to a bar at the back of the room, where people had flocked like pigeons.

Tom and Rachel were talking at the rear of Rick's booth in low and serious tones. Now Tom broke away from her, looking depressed. *Good*, I thought. *Let him suffer*. Another friend would have indulged him, asked what the matter was, but I had no patience for that. All I noticed, with a kind of relish, was a chink in the armor of a personality that had dominated me for most of the year.

I said, "You know what I think?"

"What."

"I think Miles has been putting you on. I think his whole story about Cándido is a lie. I'll bet Miles gets his drugs from some regular guy for a cheap price and has you convinced that it's all this pure cocaine, straight from Central America or whatever."

"You don't know shit," he said.

"Neither do you."

He fell silent.

Miles threaded his way back to the booth with four bottles of beer. He handed them to Rick, but Rick motioned to the rest of us. "Here you guys go," he said. Miles handed them around. "It's on me. How long can you stay, anyhow? Till like six? I might need some help behind the booth."

Tom shrugged in a way that meant yes.

"That'd be great. I'll let you know when I need a break, okay? These drinks are payment." He smirked and tilted up his beer. "You coming to my party?"

"What party?"

"I'm having a party in two weeks. Actually, my parents are having it, but I'm inviting a bunch of my friends." Rick hesitated. "I thought Rachel told you."

"Rachel hasn't told me anything."

She stood at the front of the booth now, watching other people. "Well, you're invited," said Rick. "It's a casual thing."

He tilted up his bottle again and turned to deal with a customer. Miles stood next to us, smoking thoughtfully.

"Should be a good party," he said. "Stanley Kubrick might be there."

"Hey, can I ask you something?" Tom said.

"What's up."

"Didn't you say that Flambón guy had a car dealership in Burbank?"

"Near Burbank, yeah."

"Isn't that close by? I was wondering if we could go there and buy some coke."

Miles frowned. "Well, it's over the hill, on the freeway." He smoked his cigarette and shrugged. "But I am going over in like an hour. I guess I could get you something."

"Can we go with you?"

Now Miles adjusted his sunglasses and looked out across the crowded hall. The frown on his face became more of a delicate pursing of narrow lips.

"Don't know if I can do that," he said.

"How come?"

"Flambón's touchy. Don't know if he'd be in the mood."

Tom glanced away and shook his head in wounded disbelief. Miles stared blankly through his glasses.

"Oh, hell," he said at last. "You guys aren't cops, right? Let me think about it."

He disappeared into the crowd. We didn't see him again for an hour and a half. When he turned up, looking paler than before—still nervous, twitching another cigarette between his fingers—he said, "I'm going over to see Flambón. If you want, you can come, too. But you have to stay in the car."

"Okay," we agreed.

Leaving the church was like sudden sobriety: From a haze of white-lit smoke and painted flesh we had to get used to the dry sunlight of a Los Angeles afternoon. The neighborhood felt bland and dead. Miles's decrepit brown Cadillac sat a block from the church and smelled, inside, like stale cigarette ash. He turned up some horrible synth-based music and drove us with a minimum of conversation out to Burbank.

Koreatown and Burbank lie in separate hollows of the Los Angeles basin, so we had to spend a few minutes on the rutted Hollywood Freeway. For a while there were grassy hills and brownish, almost Gothic-looking overpasses. Then we plunged into a neighborhood of dry suburban lawns and endless telephone poles, moplike palm trees, and oval supermarket signs mounted on swooping metal spires. The streets were like broad canals of asphalt.

Not everyone realizes that greater L.A. is actually a *fountainhead* of asphalt: The city lies on a bed of tar that in some places bubbles up from the ground. More than a hundred years of progress have simply pulled the stuff to the surface—by the vat, by the steaming square mile—and flooded not just the streets of L.A. but all the neighboring towns. Burbank was one of the first to go under.

Miles parked across the street from a parking lot of sad-looking cars. Strings of colored flags flicked in the wind. The dealership was called A.B.C. Used Autos.

"This is it?" Tom said.

"Yeah. Wait here." Miles swung open the Cadillac's door and we watched him jaywalk over to a boxy white office building on the edge of the lot.

Tom creased his forehead. We were expecting a car dealership, but this one looked so—ordinary. Pathetic, downtrodden, used-up, sad. We were used to Mercedes or Volvo showrooms in Calaveras Beach, places that looked sinful enough to be fronts for a money-laundering empire. The idea that we were parked outside the well-spring of so much pure Colombian coke was a little hard to grasp. How could all that jungle powder find its way to *this* particular corner of Burbank, California? It occurred to me that I didn't even know what cocaine was, much less how it was made, though now I can picture the blade-harvested hills of coca shrubs giving up tons of leaves to be leached in acid and trampled like grapes for a grey essence that oozes out like jam. I can picture the purified, powdered essence packed into bricks and smuggled over Mexico and the Caribbean in chartered planes. I can imagine a distribution system centered in a large American city, involving lots of cars that naturally need to be parked in a convenient, unlikely place. Now a great deal of this scene makes more sense than it did at the time; but in the back of Miles's Cadillac it was a steep disappointment, another tumble away from our teenage fantasy world.

I mean, *A.B.C. Used Autos?* It was almost funny.

"Big old drug dealer, huh," I said lazily.

"Shut up, Eric."

"Big old Cándido Flambón."

"Fuck you."

"Did he give you his phone number? Maybe we can call him later at his house."

"Shut *up*, will you?"

Tom turned and tapped his knee.

This would be the first of two disillusionments on that brutal afternoon. Tom's cocaine-cowboy image was so important to him that having it mocked by the banality of the car lot dealt a serious blow to his foundations, or what he thought were his foundations.

After fifteen minutes Miles came out alone and climbed into the Cadillac.

"Sorry, guys," he said. "Nothing today."

"What do you mean?" said Tom.

"He's not selling today."

"He doesn't have anything?"

Miles shrugged. "I said he could be really touchy."

We pulled away from the curb. Tom twisted in the front seat to gaze back at the lot. I gave him a sarcastic smile.

"We should have bet money."

"Shut up, Eric."

"*You* shut up. You would have lost."

"Hey, guys," Miles said.

Tom looked miserable.

xl

The crowd in the church had thinned. The only person behind Rick's booth was Amos. Leather jackets and bare chests still drifted around the hall, but the torture-chamber intensity of an hour before had mellowed into something casual and hung-over, like the aftermath of a circus. Amos said, "Hey guys, what's happening?"

"Where is everyone?" said Tom.

"Rick's taking a break. He was wondering where you guys went. He needed someone to watch the booth for a while, but you were gone."

"We went out with Miles."

"Where *is* Miles?"

"He went home."

Amos nodded and glanced at the thinning crowd. He looked tired.

"Where's Rachel?" said Tom.

"I don't know, she's around somewhere. I think she went to the bathroom." He looked in the direction of the bar and squinted. His expression fell; he looked worried. "You guys can leave, if you want. I've got things pretty much under control."

But Tom said, "Is that Rick?" and started toward the bar.

The bar area had a looping countertop. At one of the rounded corners, stretching across the vinyl to chat with a bartender, we saw Rick half-leaning on a stool, smiling with his lizard lips and holding Rachel by the waist. Rachel's head bobbed to the distorted music and her eyes gazed blankly out from under her hair. Soon she broke away from Rick, turned to say something in his ear, kissed him, and walked off to a far corner of the bar toward the bathroom.

Tom froze in place, staring. A blush crept into his chest and spread over the wedge exposed by his oversized shirt. The high color made me think of the flush in his father's face, the thick-pored ruddiness and watery-eyed look brought on by gin and wine; but Tom was young, and you could almost watch his spry body admit these feelings the way a shining motor takes in fuel. (Pain can be energizing.) I wasn't sure what to do. Tattoo needles buzzed like cicadas. I sensed a shock of emotion in my friend that hadn't really shown itself since our earliest days on the basketball court—a kind of sickening breach in his eyes, a black self-hatred and fear. I wondered if every case of heartbreak wasn't just a taste of the same awful disappointment, a realization that what you thought was ground is nothing but vapor and dust.

Tom strode up to the bar. Rick's face smiled. He wiped a strand of oiled hair from his forehead and said, "Oh, hey. What are you doing?"

Tom didn't answer.

"I was wondering where you went. I had to get Amos to watch the booth for an hour because you guys bailed."

"Have you seen Rachel?"

Now Rick's eyes retreated, calculating. He said, "No, not for a while. I think she must have gone home."

Instantly I hated him. It was a cynical fib, and his pale, smirking face had a smugness in it that disgusted me. Tom kicked a stool and seemed ready to speak, or yell, but instead he just broke a strut on the stool with his boot, and kept kicking until the wrecked thing fell over. Then he stalked past Rick toward the bathroom. I fixed Rick's eyes and said, "We *saw* her," hoping this would sound corrosive. Without waiting for an answer I went after Tom. A crooked line of people stood against a corner wall by the bathroom. The door was a narrow strip of black-painted wood. Tom stepped up to it and pounded. *Boom-boom-boom.* "RACHEL." People in line objected; a girl's voice inside said, "What the *fuck*," and I felt a combination of anger and paralyzing, mortal fear. I grabbed Tom's shoulder, but he slapped me away. "RACHEL." *Boom-boom-boom.*

The toilet flushed, the door opened. A tall, freckled woman with blond hair stared at Tom through a pair of tinted glasses. "Excuse me?" she said in a surprisingly gentle voice. "Do I know you?"

"Ah, hell."

Tom bolted. I turned to follow him across the noisy church hall and down the steps. The front door swung open, and the late-afternoon sunlight hurt my eyes. When my vision adjusted I saw Tom unlocking the Chrysler. I ran across the street and got in. Without a word, he slammed the car into gear and pulled away, nervously chirping the tires.

"Jesus, take it easy," I said.

We drove through Koreatown, through the bricklike clutter of stores. Tom punched through traffic, eyes gazing hard at the other cars, his foot heavy. We lurched past the onramp to the freeway and got lost in the tangle of streets.

I said, "Tom, pull over."

"Why?"

"Because you're driving like an asshole. And we're lost."

"We're not lost," he said in a wretched voice.

"What's the matter?" I said.

"What do you *think's* the matter?"

"Fuck, it can't be that bad."

"What do *you* know about it?"

"Could you just stop the car?"

"I'm looking for the freeway."

"It's behind us. We passed it."

"I know."

We moved forward slowly. I crossed my feet in one corner, away from the teacher's brake. A few cars had turned on their headlights, and the sky behind the buildings had turned a smoggy pink.

Suddenly I felt a wild urge to confess to Tom, to strip my conscience. The fear in me mixed with ferocious remorse over what I'd said to Rick. How could I judge him? He probably knew I'd fooled around with Rachel. Rachel had probably mentioned it. I was a hypocrite, no better than him. Pangs of guilt made me want to disappear. The neighborhood around us was a shallow cynical shell of concrete and stucco and glass, and Tom moved through it like a ravening lion, stone-faced but suffering in his nerves. I wondered what he would do when he found Rachel.

I blurted out a speech: "You know, just because Rick might be fucking her doesn't mean the world's coming to an end. It wouldn't be the worst thing that ever happened to someone, you know, it's not exactly unprecedented."

God knows what I expected. There was a long sickening silence while we sat in an intersection with the blinker on. Tom just stared at me, paper-pale. At a break in traffic, he swung the car around and sped in the opposite direction, toward the freeway. For the first time, I started to feel real terror. Tom was firmly at the wheel, but his mind was gone.

Traffic thickened; a leviathan tractor-trailer in front of us squealed its brakes. Then a few things happened at once. Across the street I saw a familiar brown-skinned shape step into a bus shelter and sit down. Rachel was waiting, I guessed, for a crosstown bus back to

Calaveras Beach. Maybe she'd seen Tom's tantrum in the church and made a run for it. Blood started to pound in my veins. Then the tractor-trailer taillights shuddered right in front of us at windshield level, and I shouted, "Tom, look out!"

He swerved left—too fast—so that suddenly the black steel bumper of the truck lunged at the windshield. I stood on the teacher's brake, feeling the need to distract Tom, to confuse him and keep him from noticing Rachel. The Chrysler bounced on its shocks. A car behind us on Tom's side rammed into the front fender and the square-ended truck bumper spiderwebbed the windshield like a hammer punching through a frozen surface. Glass chunks fell in my lap, and now I was sharing the passenger side with a corner of steel and a cracked taillight. But still no one was hurt. "You've really fucking done it now, haven't you?" I hollered. "I *told* you to pull over the car!" I slapped my knees, burning with indignation. "What do you think you're gonna do when you find her, Tom—slap her around? Punch her till she says she's sorry? You really think that every ounce of pain must be somebody else's fault, don't you, but you're nothing but a spoiled punk, okay, a suburban brat with an attitude problem—" and here Tom reached for me with both hands and rammed my head against the bumper. With one palm wrapped around my neck and the other behind my head he pounded at the steel the way you might pound at a rock with a coconut.

There was a blur of panic and a strange, instant withdrawal, as if the pain I should have been feeling belonged to somebody else. I tried to resist, but the more I fought Tom's hands, the harder he pushed. He had the strength of a wild animal. It was like a nightmare coming true. No, it was worse—like the fulfillment of something I had never even imagined, of a deep and seismic existential dread. And it happened so quickly I couldn't quite grasp my own bad luck. There were cracking noises and a pain in my skull. A corner of the bumper ripped into my neck—warmly, with a sharp sudden pain—

and I felt blood wash over my clothes in a flood, like a waiting regiment spilling into enemy territory. I jerked back. For a moment Tom's eyes looked cold and merciless, diamond-bright. Then, either from real remorse or for the benefit of the other drivers, he started to shout, "Oh my God! Oh my fucking God!" and climbed out of the car.

The pain in my head and jaw seemed to brighten my senses. I could take in details around me with a crisis-born clarity. Tom ran around the back of the Chrysler and a nervous lean man helped him with my door. Traffic was tangled; people stared from their cars. Horns blared. To the left, smoggy pink sunlight had deepened to orange, and the soft arc of sunset color bleeding into pale blue sky seemed preternaturally beautiful. But when I moved, my skull crackled like a damaged egg. My head and jaw throbbed. I held my hand to the wound. The warm wash of blood down my chest came in regular pulses, quicker than a second hand, and the flow felt like a sensual mollification or dulling of that temporary sharpness of sight. In some ways it was good to feel the warm liquid against my cooling skin.

The lean man in a flannel shirt helped me out of the car. With his and Tom's help, I stumbled to the edge of a construction site and sat down on a sandy patch of grass. The stranger asked me to lie back, but I resisted and tried to act as if everything was under control. Blood urged out of me, soaking my clothes, and my body felt weak and chill. Tom stood there looking horrified. He was like a soft-faced gunslinger, an innocent little blood-spattered Jesse James, and across the street behind him loomed a building called the Cockatoo Lounge, with a sign advertising NAKED GIRLS! NAKED GIRLS! and a massive, neon-outlined cockatoo turning on the roof. I saw more people running to help. The cockatoo, backlit by a flaming sky, looked sinister, surreal, like some evil messenger in a dream. There was an arch look on its face. It spun counterclockwise. I noticed that its dirty neon tubes were about the color of mustard. Traffic honked, strangers shouted. I looked for Rachel across the street, but the shelter was empty. Sometime during my disaster a bus must have carried her away. I couldn't believe it. The simple act of sitting up soon felt like too much work. My fingertips turned cold. A cloudiness swirled in my vision like water over the head of a drowning victim. Tom and I stared at each other one last time before I fell back with my eyes rolled into my head, and passed out on the sand patch from the sheer system-shock of sudden and awful understanding.

xli

For a while—hours, minutes—everything was black. I had no sense of time, no sense of anything. Then there was a strange stirring of some alternative consciousness, like a faint illumination in deep water. The old sensation of inhabiting a body was like a dull, distant cramp. I seemed to float over the scene of the crime and hazily saw cop cars, a tow truck, and an ambulance. Blue and amber lights flickered across the pavement. Only when I started to piece together what had happened did my senses start to clear. The fog dissipated under the force of a keen and powerful outrage. Anger scalded my senses clean, and I thought: *Wait. Is this completely irreversible?* It seemed a bit much, having to pay for a moment of rash courage with your whole life.

The strangers on the sidewalk looked casual, relaxed. They weren't behaving like people at a murder scene. Tom answered questions from two cops on the sidewalk, hands bound only by plastic restraints. The police also questioned the nervous lean man, who now smoked a cigarette, as well as an energetic old lady who wore a bathrobe and a printed polyester kerchief on her head. They gave conflicting accounts, and the cops were confused.

"Don't listen to these people, Officer," I said. "They're just distorting the record."

The cop heard nothing.

"Dammit, hey! EXCUSE ME!"—but it was no use. No one could hear me, and the thing was done. After sixteen years of shlemielhood at last Eric Sperling finally finds some faint courage of his convictions, and what does he get? *Bupkes*. Nothing. A brutal blow to the head.

part six

xlii

Our train pulls into a Stockton railyard. The sun has dropped low in the west and the air here smells like dust and grease. Rodney's been looking my way with his clouded, searing eyes for at least half an hour. Now he shakes his head and squeezes his eyes with a grimy thumb and forefinger.

"Man," he says, blinking like somebody waking from a dream.

He notices the book lying beside him in the barley, and shoves it into his pack. He crawls to the side of the car and raises his eyes above the rim. The brakes begin to shriek and the cars lurch and bang to a stop. He lies flat on the pile of grain. Soon we hear footsteps trampling through the dust, followed by a desperate scrabble against the rear of the car. "Aw, hell!" Rodney mutters, and a plump, sweating Mexican in an open plaid shirt jumps in. "Hey, amigo," he says. "They're breakin' up the train. Mind if we join you?" He turns to call something in Spanish, and three of his friends hop over the rim.

"Where you headed?" says Rodney.

"Up to Santa Rosa."

"Pickin' grapes?"

The Mexican nods, but his answer is cut short by a series of lurches and clanks reverberating through the cars. Rodney rubs his chin.

"You sure this part a the train's headed up there?"

"That's what the yard workers said."

"They mention where that other half's goin'?"

"I don't know. Sacramento?"

"Well," says Rodney. "Sacramento's more in my direction." He props himself up again to look at the railyard. "I gotta split," he says, and surprises me by disappearing over the side.

My first instinct is to follow him, to retrieve that damn book. But the idea that this train will run to Santa Rosa stays me. Guerneville's fifteen miles from Santa Rosa.

• • •

My parents committed my coffin to the ground one day after the disaster, on a mild spring morning, attended by Rabbi Gelanter and a small crowd of friends. Under the veil of her narrow hat, my mother's face looked drawn and drained. She wore a dark belted dress, black gloves, and a shawl. My dad wore charcoal wool with pinstripes; the wryness was gone from my his haggard eyes and his heavy mustache sagged. He seemed to stoop more than before. Their suffering shattered me. Doug and Doug stood with their parents in the solemn congregation, wearing navy suits. Greta Linden stood nearby in a black skirt-and-blazer ensemble. A mound of soil was lumped next to the grave for my parents to scoop with a hand shovel, and my dad ceremonially tossed the first few clods of earth. Then my mom took the shovel and tried to spoon a little dirt down the hole, but she was fragile and distracted. After three small shovelfuls, she gave up.

• • •

The red sun in the west has washed the sky with an orange-yellow tint by the time our train pulls away. The lazing migrant workers yawn and scratch their bellies. They must be wiped out from a day of travel. Or else they're storing up strength: I guess a normal day's work for these guys must be more strenuous than train-hopping. I consider this for a while. Wheels clack under the railroad car for minutes on end until the surprising thought arises—like a simple recognition—that their lives have been harder than mine.

• • •

But Tom got off easy. That's the problem, possibly the whole reason I've stuck around since that horrible day. Tom spent three years in Juvenile Hall and two in state prison. His trial was a short and formal affair between a public prosecutor and the public defender, Mr. O'Connor. The only spectators were Greta Linden, my parents, and a reporter from the *Strand Bulletin*. Greta wore her finest outfit, a white-trimmed purple suit with matching hat, normally reserved for weddings, which made her seem regal and alien to Tom, as if her high formality was a way of disowning him. She didn't mean to send such a stark message, but the distance she achieved with her purple suit was the only way to deal with her warring emotions.

Tom sat granite-eyed in court. He listened to the prosecutor's droning accusations and wallowed in the rich slop of evidence that Society—bland, conformist, suit-wearing, automatic—was biased against him. The chief prosecutor *did* have a murder case, but it was weak, and my parents never asked him to push it. As a witness, he called up the driver of the car that slammed into us, who said he watched Tom hammer my head into the truck bumper. This guy was an unshaven, unemployed character with insurance-related motivations for lying, and he failed to convince the jury. Mr. O'Connor countered his testimony with a witness of his own, who declared from the stand in a bright, clear voice that she saw exactly what the police and the papers had reported.

This was Mrs. Wheeler, the woman in the polyester head-kerchief.

"You were on the sidewalk at the time?" Mr. O'Connor asked.

"Yes sir, I saw it all from the side of the street."

"Which side?"

"Well, the side they were on. Near the building site."

"And what did you see?"

In a flat, brash, precise old voice, she said, "I didn't see anything until I heard truck brakes beside me as I was walkin' along, and when I turned to see, a car was comin' down the street too fast for traffic. And right in front of it, there was the truck. I seen the car swerve to miss, then that gentleman's car come up from behind and bashed it in the truck bumper. I seen the boy go forward and knock his head."

"Did you take note of the driver?"

"Well, he *did* seem distraught."

"Did you see him attack the victim?"

"No, he never touched him."

Mrs. Wheeler's testimony was enough to cancel the other witness's, because to the jury she seemed to have no personal interest in coming forward. But I understood that she was the sort of neighborhood busybody who likes to be involved in any excitement on the street, offering opinions, helping the cops, and later appearing on a witness stand (should this be called for) holding the attention of a hushed courtroom. Her testimony swayed the verdict toward manslaughter.

The trial took all of two weeks. In the end Tom went to jail for grand theft auto, driving without a license, driving under the influence, manslaughter, and finally—with an affidavit from his stoic, brokenhearted mother—for breaking and entering.

xliii

Guerneville amounts to a bend in the road where shops and an old cinema rise like a hedge at the feet of some ancient, towering redwoods. Tom has lived in his creaky flat here for three years. His tiny eyes have deepened under his low, straight brow, his blond hair has burnished a little, and he looks at people with a challenging, blaming glare. The lithium treatments in jail put weight on his narrow frame and turned him sluggish. His interviews with a psychologist in prison also rehashed the story of our car accident in the same old fictional detail, so by the time he walked free, in 1989, Tom could pretend that five years had been stolen from him by mishap, blind fate, or even conspiracy, as if government prosecutors and parole officers had plotted to rob him of part of his youth. His mood still swings between wallows of self-pity and an almost Nietzschean will to dominate, the old blank-faced insistence that the world view Tom Linden as Tom Linden views himself.

It's this willful stubbornness that pisses me off. He lives by a myth of himself as a largely innocent man, ill-treated by the state's legal system but fighting his way back, forging ahead like a captain on the deck of a storm-tossed ship.

The road to Guerneville is deserted at this hour. The sky is a thick spray of icy stars, and great fields of grass and stands of trees give off an earthy, fertile smell. Tom lives above a shop called Williams Hardware, in a building with washed-out plank siding and stairs running up on the right. An aluminum screen door is attached to the frame at the top of the stairs, so my first trick as I slip inside is to swing the screen door wide and let it slam. The smack disturbs the damp silence like a dull cymbal crash, and I hear Tom shift in bed.

Not much has changed. Heavy brown paint on the floorboards, dusty aluminum blinds. A Formica bar separates the kitchen from the living room, which is cluttered with newspapers and an old pizza box. Dishes lie unwashed in the sink. It still looks like a bachelor pad. The last time I visited, two years ago, Tom's girlfriend was Jessie Williams, the landlord's daughter. She thought of herself as a rehabilitating angel, possibly a future wife. But for Tom she was just a fling. Most of his life since jail has been lonely and rootless, and he seems to like it that way. He learned basic house carpentry in jail; when a building boom started in northern California he settled in an apartment and helped to girdle small wine-country towns with tract homes and condominiums. First he lived in Santa Rosa, because most of the work was concentrated in that part of Sonoma County. But after rents began to rise he moved fifteen miles west, to Guerneville.

Jessie was an innocent blond town girl with a strong imagination, who filled the gaps in Tom's life story with details worthy of a romantic, wandering carpenter. She was younger than Tom but treated him like a boy, or like a doll that required discipline. In her long slim body and wide-set eyes a stranger could read innocence, trust, and girlish devotion. In her long but shapeless blond hair, and in her crooked smile, there were suggestions of man-weary cyni-cism. I liked her; in spite of myself, I thought she was good for Tom. But he didn't always think so.

Impatience with Jessie and with his drowsy life in Guerneville drove him now and then to San Francisco, where he could visit strip joints and troll for other women in bars. I thought of those trips as odd gestures of hope. Tom wanted a new life in the city, some kind of change. San Francisco by this time—about 1997—was growing as frenetic as downtown L.A., and the heavy traffic frightened him. (It seemed to give him bad memories.) Whenever he drove in for an afternoon, he would park his truck and use public transportation. His life in Guerneville was a kind of exile, an obscure penance away from teeming crowds, but San Francisco was society itself, and on the buses and streetcars on weekends he mingled with preening hip-sters, starchy professional women, pushy Chinese ladies, swaggering gangsters, transvestites, hustlers, and madmen.

Tom wanted to fit in. He wanted a job, or a new girlfriend, or some reason to live in town. So he developed a San Francisco persona: On top of his glowery backwoods face he laid a chipper, optimistic veneer. He bought Hawaiian prints and some comfortable deck shoes. He learned to say, "You bet," and pat strangers on the arm. He arched his eyebrows with an earnest, Dean Martin show of surprise, instead of a sneering squint. The effect was weird, and strangers were never sure whether to feel offended. No one he saw in San Francisco had ever met Joe Linden, which meant that no one recognized how eerily Tom's persona had drifted into an impression—almost a sarcastic impersonation—of his dad.

How did he get this way? How did such a strong-willed, nervy kid become so thick and dull? The simple answer is prison, which hardened Tom on a few different levels. He put on muscle in the prison gym, which toughened him physically. The layers of fabrication blunting the crime on his conscience also grew thick and bulbous. And his personality changed from quick and intense to stubborn and overbearing. If he'd started to think in simple terms of power and rebellion in high school, prison only strengthened his prejudices, and he learned to despise authority with a sickening immediate hatred aimed at anyone wearing a uniform.

But he did have a conversation in state prison that struck deep enough below Tom's hide to work a slow, almost chemical change. He told Jessie about it one night on the couch in his living room. There was rain outside; they were smoking pot, and a movie called *Air America* was on TV. During a commercial, Tom stretched on the sofa lazily and said, "Did I ever tell you about the drug pilot I met in jail?"

"I don't think so."

"He ran drugs like these guys." He nodded at the television. "He knew Cándido Flambón." (Jessie had heard all about Flambón.) "One time I was mouthing off about him in the chow hall, bragging a little I guess, and a middle-aged guy with ugly scarred-up cheeks says: 'Flambón? I used to fly planes for him. How'd you meet him?'

"At first I was embarrassed, 'cause everyone at the table could hear. I think this guy's gonna make me look dumb. So I say, 'I just sold for him sometimes. I didn't ever really meet him. There was a middle guy.'

"And he says, 'Flambón had government protection.'

"I asked him what he meant, government protection. He said all the pilots he knew were protected by the federal government. Flambón's whole operation was protected. They flew in planeloads of coke to the U.S. with immunity from the CIA. The government knew the coke was headed to Florida, Arkansas, California. He said he dealt with federal agents.

"Bull*shit*," said Jessie.

"Well, that's what he told me. He said it was like a business relationship. Flambón belonged to this network to raise money for his political friends—that much I already knew. And when the government decided his friends could help, they made a deal. The CIA did. This pilot said the CIA greased the wheels of this drug operation to help the *Contras* fight communism."

Jessie looked incredulous, and Tom gave a hollow, mocking laugh. "I couldn't believe it either. But no one else at the table was laughing, so I shut my mouth. This was in, like, 1987, when the Iran-*Contra* hearings were on TV. I always figured the president was some old grandfather who wouldn't know a line of coke from his own rear end."

Jessie laughed; Tom smiled. But he never got over the strangeness of the pilot's story. Beyond Rick, beyond Miles, beyond the underworld cabal of Cándido Flambón, stood, in some capacity, the smiling, waving figure of President Reagan. Was it possible? Tom had always liked to think of himself as a dangerous outsider, a navigator of unofficial seas, but now he saw himself, for the first time, as a pawn.

"So anyway, this pilot got up from the table. He said, 'Don't worry about it, kid, no one else knows this shit, either. It's Ollie North's big secret.' He kind of nodded up at the TV in the chow hall. Then he said he wasn't even in for smuggling coke. Local cops caught him selling in some bar in Oakland, and busted him for possession."

xliv

Crickets chirp in the grass outside; Tom whimpers and flinches in bed. The silence of the summer night feels massive around the apartment, like a heavy presence. Tom's on his back, one arm on his chest and the other out over the floor, and lying with one arm across my murderer's naked hips is his girlfriend, Jessie. Dungarees and tennis shoes, underclothes and empty bottles of liquor are tumbled at the base of the bed. The smell of sex and whiskey is strong.

Outside the window looms a curved edge of the darkened WILLIAMS HARDWARE sign, and through the leaves of an ash tree a lamp on the sidewalk throws a weird silvery shine. During my last visit to Guerneville, I never saw Tom suffer a bad night's sleep. I remember him telling Jessie, "A psychologist I had in jail taught me how to make peace with my problems. He told me I could just make the decision to feel good. That works pretty much all the time now— just knowing I can be okay with how I am. It's weird how you need permission, isn't it? I've learned to control most of my self-hatred."

"That's *great*, Tom."

"Yeah, I've learned to like myself."

Conversations like this one sent me ricocheting off the walls, because the context—always—was the lie he'd concocted in jail. Tom had told Jessie all about the "car accident." He allowed her to be his girlfriend, in fact, because she validated this nonsense about his past. Two years ago, there was nothing I could do about it. He was an ugly bastard in full denial. I wanted him to sizzle in the flames of some old-fashioned hell, wrinkle-skinned and screaming, bones crackling like firewood, until he recognized what a miserable, arrogant, reckless, bone-headed little shit he'd been—I wanted to torture his conscience with memories of what he did to me on that ugly late afternoon—and all he ever did was pass out on the sofa like an exhausted suburban dad.

But something's changed. The apartment wasn't so squalid before. Is that the difference? The mess in this room is the work of a dedicated alcoholic, not just a man who likes to binge. The bookshelf piled with magazines and the ragged armchair in the corner, the peeling brown paint, the unwashed clothes, the general indifference to how the place looks, as if Tom lived not in an apartment but in a cheap hotel—it all gives off a depressing odor of booze.

Jessie snuffles and turns on to her back. A huge bird flutters its wings outside the window and lands on a telephone wire. An owl or a crow. The vague shadow swings behind the branches of the ash. A wind stirs the trees, then dies and leaves behind that massive, throbbing, country stillness: Crickets in the yard, and from the sluggish river across the highway rises the faint creaking of frogs.

For one minute, I feel pity. Tom hasn't exactly prospered as an adult. Maybe all his mistakes and self-deceptions are excusable, understandable. Maybe I should leave him alone.

He shifts, moans, and opens his eyes.

His face has the pouchy look of a sleepwalker. He rubs his nose and squints, but I can't say whether he's dreaming or awake. I stand, by my own reckoning, about three yards from the bed, next to a pile of laundry. What I look like won't have changed since the day I was killed. I seem to have on a pair of brown shorts and a blue flannel shirt. Heavy eyebrows, pale skin. My hair is tousled and dark, unbloodied but faintly touched, right now, by the edge of the streetlight's moonlike shine.

The bird flutters away from the wire, and I flinch. A floorboard under my foot gives up a gentle groan.

"Oh my God."

Um, hi.

"Oh my fucking God."

Sorry Tom. Didn't mean to barge in while you had company.

He wails faintly from the back of his throat. Then his naked body curls on the mattress, racked with spasms of weeping. Jessie stirs awake and rubs her face. "What's the matter?"

Get the fuck out! he hollers in a deep voice, and Jessie meets this outburst with a confused and brittle silence.

After a minute, she gets up to look for her clothes on the floor.

"Where are you going?" he says.

"You just said to leave."

Tom gives another little cry and lies with one arm thrown across his face. When Jessie switches on the light, he points with his other arm at the middle of the room.

"Who's standing right there?"

"What do you mean?"

Tom doesn't answer.

"Oh—" says Jessie, coming back to the bed. "You're having an episode again, aren't you?" He keeps the arm across his eyes. Jessie kneels next to him and touches his elbow. "Take a look now, in the light. Can you see anything?"

Tom looks. "No."

"So it was a nightmare."

"I guess."

"You need a glass of water? Or can I get you something out of the bathroom? You need your meds or something?"

"I'm all out."

"Tom! You said you wouldn't do that again! No wonder you're hallucinating! *Jesus!* What was it this time? Frogs?"

He shakes his head.

"Mosquitoes?"

"No."

"Blood all over the floor?"

Tom says nothing, but covers his eyes with his arm, as if the electric light were a living plague. Jessie watches him for a moment, then moves for the doorway.

"Okay," she says. "I have to pee. Light on or off?"

"Off."

She pads to the bathroom. Tom lies still. He's suffering; maybe he's started to feel a twinge of guilt. The anger in me is gleeful, almost bloodthirsty, and my vengeance rises like the back of a challenged cat. Some kind of triumphant music should play in the background. He's realizing, I hope, how lost he is.

This alcoholic clutter stands for the squandering of two lives, not just one. Tom killed me, so now he's going down the drain. And for what, exactly? The plain uselessness of it makes me sick. You could say Tom was heartbroken by Rachel, you could point to the death of his dad, or the abuse by Harold and his friends, or the influence of *A Clockwork Orange*. You could even say that for a while he was out of his mind and wanted me not to exist. But at the bottom of this pile of explanations there's an ugly, staring void, an emptiness that swallows reason, and nothing can really account for why Tom took it upon himself to crack open my head and rob me of a long, abundant life.

This emptiness unsettles me more than anything else. It upsets my control. I actually seem to float a little on a fume of rage. I drift close to Tom's wooden bookshelf and in a seizure of grief and frustration I grab it by the edge and tilt it onto the floor. His magazines topple out. The heavy thing comes down with an apartment-shivering crash. Tom runs to the doorway. I start kicking his laundry around. In the corner close to his bed there's a table with a stereo system and a few stacks of compact discs—Limp Bizkit, Green Day, Rage

Against the Machine—which I smash and scatter in pieces across the hardwood. Then I swing from the light fixture. Tom flips the switch, and for a moment five bulbs in frosted-glass hoods send a blaze of light lurching along the walls, but I yank on the fixture by the chain until the cord pulls out and everything falls with a spectacular smash of lightbulbs and frosted glass, shorted sparking electrical wires and clanking brass, and the room goes dark again, except for the shine from outside. To an alcoholic, the weird show must seem like a bad case of delirium tremens.

Plaster dust drifts from the ceiling. Leaf shadows quiver on the floor. I feel kind of silly. But my B-movie act of revenge seems to have worked: Tom is really terrified. The screen door slams and his feet clatter on the steps. Jessie appears at the doorway, then runs after him. I sit and wait. A fresh odor of moss and slow river water wanders through the window and I feel swamped with a strange emotion. All my senses have opened, like pores. The tightness of my old urge for revenge has slackened into something like compassion.

xlv

Tom crosses the gravel to his pickup. He slams the door and starts the engine, but not before Jessie runs up to the window and says, "What was that all about, Tom? Where are you going?"

"I need a pharmacy."

"At Safeway? They're not open yet."

"I'll find one."

"But you can't go out like that—just look at yourself. You're not dressed!"

"I have clothes in the truck."

"What clothes?"

"After-work clothes," he says, and spins his tires in the gravel.

The sky has lightened over the road to the east. Tom turns on the radio. He's wearing a dingy white T-shirt and boxer shorts and thick socks. His dark blond hair sticks up in the back, and his eyes have a bleary squint. He taps the wheel and sings under his breath. I'm in the passenger seat, next to him. He doesn't seem to notice. I appear to him in fits, I guess, the way I did to Rodney.

At a cloverleaf, next to a southbound on-ramp, he pulls off the road. Tall, rich-smelling grass on the shoulder is heavy and cool. Tom half-opens the door and produces a bundle of clothes from behind his seat. These are just makeshift, after-work clothes—old khakis and a Hawaiian print, a pair of sneakers—which look dryer-shrunk and slightly too small. He puts them on, trying not to step in the damp grass, then climbs back into the truck. He rifles through the glove compartment for a slip of paper, and stuffs it in his pocket.

Now what? Things feel out of my control. The sun rises over vineyards and grassy fields; the air is moist and warm. In the countryside it should be a healthy summer day. Tom immerses himself in the speed of the truck, the lazy turning of the road, and for a while it seems as if his nerves have relaxed. His desperation eases, and the first warmth of the sun seems to lighten his mood. I can't help noticing that we don't stop at any pharmacies.

The promise of bright weather vanishes the closer we get to San Francisco, and at the Golden Gate Bridge a thick fog settles. Grassy hills beside the highway vanish upward into a bright grey murk. The city is invisible across the water, although foghorns bellow in long deep notes from the waterfront.

Tom parks in his usual spot, behind a restaurant. He boards a crowded bus. This carries him to Market Street. Nothing's open there at this hour besides a doughnut shop and a strip club. Tom buys an apple fritter and a cup of coffee, sits for a while in the shop, and reads a newspaper. Outside, next to a half-dead sycamore planted by the curb, a slim young fiddler plays reels with a fraying bow.

When breakfast is over, Tom stands and looks for a pay phone. From his pocket he takes the slip of paper, which has a number on it. The phone is bolted into the wall next to the shop, and he stands over it like a bookie, face crooked into the receiver.

"Hey," he says finally, in a low voice that's hard to interpret. "It's Tom." One end of his mouth smiles, or winces. "Can you see me before work?"

Traffic honks; the fog seems thicker.

"I'm right downtown. On Market. You just said to call if I ever needed to. . . . Yeah, it's pretty important. . . . Can we just meet like before, at the doughnut place?"

Foghorns call from the water. He bends his face to listen.

"I don't care. Bring her along."

Tom goes back into the shop and orders another coffee. He finds a seat at a table outside and reads the paper for half an hour before a woman pushing a stroller stops in front of him. At first I don't know who she is. In a dark hooded coat over a black vest, and a black T-shirt, with polished wooden beads around her neck and bright silver bangles on her wrists—in a sober, slightly funky activist's outfit, with musical jewelry—she looks like no one I recognize. The baby is brownish and wrinkled. Instead of a coffeeish highlight in the woman's bangs, there are two or three crooked strands of grey, but the smile is still brilliant, Gypsylike.

Rachel!

"Hey."

"Hey."

They greet each other with a stiff hug. The baby fusses, so Rachel sits and pushes the stroller back and forth.

"This is her?" Tom says.

"Yeah, her name's Eva."

"How old is she?"

"Ten months." Rachel smiles. Tom leans over to let the baby take his finger. She does, but glances up at Rachel.

"What's her daddy's name?"

"Joseph. He works in Oakland, for a legal-defense fund." Rachel studies Tom's face, and grows serious. "So what's this about, anyway? Are you in trouble?"

Tom shrugs. "Well, when we saw each other before, you said if I ever needed help—" He takes a deep breath and scowls at his shoes, then shakes his head. "I think I had an episode this morning."

"What does that mean?"

"A psychotic episode?"

Rachel hesitates. "That sounds serious. Shouldn't you should see a doctor?"

Tom shakes his head. "Can't we just talk for a while?"

"Sure." It is, after all, why she's here. She glances at her watch. "I have a client meeting at nine-thirty. We can talk. I just need to eat breakfast first."

They go inside and settle at a small table near the window of the doughnut shop, and Tom offers Rachel coffee. He looks bulky and buffoonish in his Hawaiian shirt, and walks as if the floor were brittle, but the simple presence of his ex-girlfriend seems to slacken his pretension. For an hour they talk about the recent past. Rachel chews her fingernail and studies him with shining black eyes. She still has the same unguarded mannerisms: The brusqueness in the way she speaks has grown husky, maternal—moralistic as opposed to sassy—but she still has to chew on something, girlishly, as he tells her about his construction work in Sonoma. Rachel seems stand-offish and treats Tom like a charity case, but when she goes into her own troubles after high school—drinking, community college, then two years at UCLA—it's hard not to notice how strident she's become in her politics. Something in her has stiffened. After Tom went to jail she had emotional problems, either because of my death, or because of Tom's abuse, or both. What saved her was law school. And political activism. And motherhood, of course. These various forms of devotion. "My two years at law school were the first two good years of my life," she says.

"Were they?"

"I loved it. Most people don't. But I was good at it. I went right here, in the city."

Tom sips his coffee. Rachel has a career; she's showing herself off as a success in the world. She's gentle about it, not bitter, but there's a buried implication that her new sense of purpose is connected with having managed to free herself from him.

"Do you ever think about Eric?" says Tom.

"Sometimes. Sure. Why?"

The fiddler's reel skips from down the street.

"It's kind of why I called you," he says.

Rachel's forehead creases. She looks sympathetic. "I guess that must be a lot to carry around on your conscience," she says, but Tom isn't having any part of her pity.

"I could say the same thing to you."

"What does that mean?"

"It wasn't exactly an accident."

"What wasn't?"

Her eyes widen. Tom hesitates. For a moment he looks like a cornered animal, unsure of how he got to this point. Then he relaxes and begins to tell the story in an altered voice. He's still defensive, but a quiet monotone is at least more honest than a cheerful strain.

Outside, a bus on Market stirs the fog. Memories of everything that happened between them, conscious and unconscious, spoken and not—memories of everything I've mentioned, and a lot that I haven't—seem to play around the table like music. What exactly happened between them has never been clear to me. My feelings for

Rachel were always a lot stronger than my grasp of the facts, and in a sense I was a victim of my own stupid ardor.

"I'm sorry, Tom. That's awful," Rachel says when he's finished. Tom nods in silence, gazing at his feet as if the awfulness of it has never fully occurred to him before. Traffic thickens on Market, and people dressed for work hurry in and out of the shop.

After a while, Rachel adds, "But you're not trying to blame it on me, are you?"

"What? No."

"It sounds like you are." She watches him, then changes course. "You're pretty calm about it. Don't you feel any regret?"

He shakes his head. "I don't know. Sometimes at night, I do. But most of the time, not really."

"How come?"

"Well, the guys I met in state prison, the guys who'd committed murder, said they were pretty much crazy when it happened. Just gone. I think I felt the same way." He shrugs again. "Something came over me."

"Did you ever apologize to his parents?"

"In court, sure."

"But that was for the car accident," Rachel says in a rising voice. "They still think it was a car accident!"

"Yeah."

"So isn't that wrong?"

Tom's face hardens. He pauses, lowers his eyes. "It's just old history now," he says. "There's nothing I can do. It sucks, but that's all."

"So you *do* regret it."

"What do you mean?"

"You wish it hadn't happened."

"Of course I wish it hadn't happened!" Tom widens his troubled eyes and shakes his head in disbelief. "Jesus, of course I do."

"Well, that's regret."

He nods, slowly, and shifts on the seat. "I just don't feel much of anything, you know? You're supposed to feel all this guilt or sadness or whatever, and I don't feel much of anything. But it's not like I'm *happy* about Eric. I haven't been really happy for years."

"Oh, no?"

He folds his arms. "It's not that I've been miserable or sad all the time. I've just been dead. Part of me's been dead."

"Is that Eric's fault?"

"What?"

"You blame it on Eric. Like he took something from you."

"Well, he fucked my girlfriend behind my back and then pretended he could judge me."

The remark is both a question and an accusation, leveled at Rachel. From the bitterness in his voice I suspect he's been waiting a long time to say it to her, or to anyone. How much did he know, I wonder? How did he find out?

Rachel returns Tom's wounded stare with a cool one of her own. ". . . And he could make you feel like such a—"

"But you killed him, Tom."

"—an *idiot*. That's what it was. He always tried to put you down. He got to be a sarcastic little bastard there at the end."

"But you killed him."

"What?"

"Maybe you lost control, went crazy or whatever, but nobody forced you, right? You killed him." She hesitates, then gets personal: "You can't give me this bullshit about, 'Oh, I was so upset because of Rachel and Rick, I had to get in a car accident and kill Eric.' Like it's my fault? No. No way."

Tom stares at her fiercely, ready to answer back. But she's basically right, even if no one has put it like this to his face before. The fact of my murder has never been quite real to him, because it was never real to anyone else. Tom disentangles his arms and sags a little in the chair. I think he was hoping to ease his conscience by telling Rachel the truth; maybe he wanted advice on turning himself in. But that isn't what he got. He stares at her and absorbs the idea that all his life he's been something besides a luckless, ill-treated man. An inkstain of grief seems to smear behind his eyes. Dull grey light leaks in from the window, laying strange shadows on his face. The fiddle music outside skips and spins. Traffic moves back and forth in the street while a foghorn calls like a drowning bird, and no one says anything for a while.

xlvi

Tom and Rachel split up on Market after nine o'clock. Rachel disappears with her stroller toward a downtown office building; Tom wanders the other way, toward a bus. The Hawaiian shirt has twisted and bunched under his windbreaker and he walks along the sidewalk in a sluggish dream, looking swamped and dull.

For the length of Van Ness, on the bus, Tom sits blank-eyed against the rear of his seat. The engine strains uphill. He rises mechanically at his stop, steps off, and moves with the stiffness of a sleepwalker toward the restaurant where he's parked his truck.

He drives across the hazy bridge. Three or four cars honk and flash their headlights because his headlights aren't on. He doesn't care. His face clenches with absent rage and he starts to swear to himself. He follows the bridge across the water and into the Marin tunnel. Other drivers honk in the tunnel just because it's a tunnel. Tom releases a stream of filthy language and starts to rock back and forth, back and forth, insistently, in his seat, swaying to some frantic rhythm in his head.

Hey, Tom?

"Mtherfckr."

Tom.

"Mtherfcking SHIT!"

Last night this might have felt like sweet revenge, but now I just feel sick. Insanity wasn't really the idea. I wanted to see grief and remorse, not a total breakdown. I can't handle responsibility for a total breakdown.

Tom, buddy.

"Go to HELL."

When a gust from a tractor-trailer buffets his truck, Tom yells back with a wild bark, which he sustains for half a minute, leaning his foot on the gas.

High fog has moved across the north counties from the basin of Sausalito to the redwoods around Guerneville. The country that far north turns boggy and green: A mixture of salt air and gentle rain gives the forest a morphine quality. Moss-furred branches grow sidelong to the road, rotting in the fog, and the shaggy, deep-furrowed columns of redwoods impose a cathedral-like calm. They also cast a deep shade, and day and night there merge indistinctly with the same narcotic blurriness that infuses everything else. Even before noon on a summer morning, the woods are shadowy and grey. The road is wet, too, with quick, dangerous curves, so a care-less driver with his foot heavy on the gas could easily slip off the side.

Tom falls quiet before he reaches these woods. He no longer rocks in place or yells, but sits still and drives with a stony expres-sion. I wonder what's on his mind, if anything. Is he worried about his future? Does he wish the baby in Rachel's stroller were his daughter, instead of some guy named Joseph's? Maybe he's brooding about me, allowing his brain to revive old memories until they move on their own, reintroducing himself to some dark, unwelcome knowledge. Or, just possibly, his mind is a blank. Maybe after his storm of temper, Tom is as unreflective as his dad was by the rail of that fishing boat, as mentally casual as a man at sundown, strolling on the deck with a drink.

In any case, below Guerneville, he does slide off the shoulder, after losing traction on a curve. I slip out of the truck in time to watch it shudder into a redwood and crumple, swing around with its tail, and explode. A simple, almost natural act of violence, ending in flame. The bright oil fire illuminates the sodden trees, which are too wet to burn. It's as if the impervious forest has claimed a hoary debt. From above I watch the dancing flames and thick oil smoke with a pity that takes me by surprise. Instead of anger, or satisfaction, I feel a deep melancholy. Cars assemble around the burning truck; people get out with cell phones. Traffic snarls. Someone has a fire extinguisher. The firemen take too long to arrive; an ambulance takes even longer. The extinguisher's tiny plume doesn't help. Drivers trade stories about what they've seen, but no one can describe the actual event. Even if they could, it would make no difference. The newspapers will call it an accident.

• • •

What do I feel now? Regret? No, not quite. But I still wonder why this death of mine had to be such an opera consisting of Eric Sperling's senseless tragedy and his long, extended gripe. It occurs to me that maybe I had a guilty conscience. Is it possible? Sure, it's possible. Guilt is the lowest feeling in the emotional toilet; it rips into self-esteem, and therefore has to be denied. This rule goes for a victimized *nefesh* like me as well as criminals or kings. Out beyond my narrow point of view there's a whole universe of things, a teeming empire of possibility, which I feel kind of stupid for not noticing before. Tom was right—around him I could be sneaky and spiteful, treacherous and cruel. I fucked his girlfriend. He knew about it—or anyway suspected it—and suffered. My sins may be skimpy compared to murder, but I've never let them assume their own shape in my mind, and part of me seems to cool or diminish at the idea that all this time I've spent outlining my grievances I've also thought of myself as the kid underneath, the white-hearted murderee.

• • •

The sky deepens. Stars prick through the night-blue vault and the moon looks hard as a bone. I lift myself high enough to take in the surrounding hills and the glow of lights from San Francisco. Surf sloshes on the coast a few miles off, and in the gathering silence of twilight it sounds insistent, irresistible. The salt air seems to erode me into something mysterious and unrecognizable. The moon is bright but narrow, not like a round stone but like a glowing bird rib, curved and bleached. It's magnificent when you think about it—that the sliver of moon we see is only a shadow-projection formed by a pair of whirling rocks, and that the moon itself may have been part of the earth before it got blasted away by a comet, long ago. The debris formed into a cluster of cold dead crust—goes the theory— and the core started to burn with slow radioactive decay. The clod of crust settled into its swing around the earth, and its ghostly face has been sliding in and out of our sunlight ever since, unerratic, like a pale but abiding companion born of an ancient wound.

Author's Note

For the parts of this book dealing with the Zohar's breakdown of the soul, I've relied on two translations of the Zohar itself, a brief but helpful conversation with Henry Falkenberg in San Francisco, Joshua Trachtenberg's *Jewish Magic and Superstition*, Gershom Scholem's Major Trends in Jewish Mysticism, Herbert Weiner's *9 1/2 Mystics*, and Alan Unterman's excellent *Dictionary of Jewish Lore and Legend.* It goes without saying that the novel is just a gloss on old ideas that run very deep. Any distortions, departures from tradition, or outright mistakes are mine.

For the historical bits having to do with Contra drug smuggling and the CIA, I'm indebted to Gary Webb's *Dark Alliance*, Alfred McCoy's *The Politics of Heroin*, Alexander Cockburn and Jeffrey St. Clair's *Whiteout*, transcriptions from Senator John Kerry's 1988 "Senate Committee Report on Drugs, Law Enforcement, and Foreign Policy," and several articles from the Allen Ginsberg archive at Stanford University's Department of Special Collections.

Calaveras Beach is a fictional town that shares a few street names with the South Bay section of L.A. county. All characters are imaginary.

Thanks also to: my fine editor Tina Pohlman, Daniel Greenberg, Miek Coccia, Nate Knaebel, Joe Loya for vetting the prison scenes, Blanche Schwappach, Ethan Watters, Matt and Jennifer Humphrey, Marc Levy, Christine Gasparac for an anecdote, and of course my wife, Jennifer Bullock.

M.S.M.

About the Author

MICHAEL SCOTT MOORE is a reporter and chief stage critic for *SF Weekly* in San Francisco. He has also written for Salon.com, *San Francisco* magazine, *Bostonia* magazine, and the *New York Times*, and runs a web site at radiofreemike.com. He lives in San Francisco.